LOCKSET

University Square, Book Two

Brenda Murphy

A NineStar Press Publication

www.ninestarpress.com

Lockset

Printed in the USA

Print ISBN: 978-1-64890-120-1

First Edition, October, 2020

Also available in eBook, ISBN: 978-1-64890-119-5

WARNING:

This book contains sexually explicit content, which may only be suitable for mature readers, death of a parent, homophobia, references to drug addiction, and infidelity.

To C, always, thank you for always believing.

Chapter One

Eunice Park glared at the ringing phone on her desk. On the third ring she picked it up. "What is it?"

"Sorry to bother you, Eunice, but your father's on the line. He insisted I connect him."

Eunice leaned forward and straightened her posture. "What?"

"Your father. Says it's urgent. Want me to take a message? Or leave him on hold till he hangs up?"

Eunice swept her hair back with one hand and closed her fist around it, barely resisting the urge to tear it out. "No. I'll talk to him." She took her reading glasses off and tossed them on the top of the stack of trial transcripts and depositions on her desk.

"Eun?" James Park's rich baritone filled her ear. Her Korean name, spoken in the way it was meant to be said, made her heart squeeze. She detested Eunice and still cursed the day she had chosen to use it instead of her true name.

"Yes." She pinched the bridge of her nose. "It's me."

Silence stretched out between them, harsh and violent. Eun settled back into her chair. Her father's silence and its power over Eun had weakened over the years. Eun knew his trick. Wait for the other to become so uncomfortable they spilled their secrets and told you everything you wanted to know. For once, Eun would not give in. She set her gaze on the clock on her computer screen. One minute. Two minutes. Eun fiddled with the edge of her blotter.

At three and one-half minutes her father cleared his throat and spoke. "Come home. I need to see you."

"Nothing's changed." Eun chewed her lip.

"I need to see you."

"Why now? I'm not coming home to be berated again. You made yourself clear five years ago. I'm not backing down. Not this time."

"I'm not asking you to. I have something to discuss with you. I can't do it over the phone. Please. This weekend?"

Eun rubbed her forehead. "I can't. I'm buried. I have dog of a case, my cocounsel is an idiot, and I've got closing arguments next week. The weekend after?"

"If that's the best you can do."

"What?" Eun's voice rose as anger she had managed to contain bubbled up. "Oh hell no. You can't call me up out of the blue, demand I see you, and then act all pissy if I can't drop what I'm doing and run home. Not after what you pulled last time. I'm lesbian, Dad. I've been lesbian, I'm going to be lesbian. Nothing is going to change that."

"I know." The defeated tone in his voice scraped against Eun's battered heart.

"I have to go."

"Will you come?"

"Next weekend."

Her father disconnected the call. Eun fell back into her chair. Late afternoon sun raked the tops of the high-rise buildings surrounding the office building. Red-and-orange light, reflected off the glass, shone through the floor to ceiling window and glinted off the framed print on the wall opposite her desk.

Her stomach rumbled, an audible reminder of her neglecting to eat breakfast and lunch. She tapped her pen on the desk and glowered at the stack of transcripts on her desk as she rang her assistant. "Order us some food, please.'

"Have a hankering for anything?" Sally's soft drawl spilled through the phone.

"Whatever you want."

"You okay?"

"I will be." Eun spun her pen in a circle, a wave of guilt for keeping her assistant after hours swept over her. "You don't have to stay. John must miss you."

"He does. But he also knows how important this case is. Faizal's okay?"

"Sounds wonderful. That gyro salad they do."

"Baklava too?"

Eun's mouth watered at the thought of the sticky honey-sweet dessert. "Of course."

"On it."

Eun hung up and spun in her chair to face her bookshelf. The black-framed photo of Eun and her father at her law school graduation was opposite a photo of Eun and her mother at Eun's kindergarten graduation. She closed her eyes as the memory of the last fight she'd had with her father surfaced. Anger and humiliation over his demand she go to conversion therapy surged through her as strong and as raw as that evening. Memories of other interventions, his relentless set-ups with eligible young men, and the shocked expressions of his church friends when she told them all the only thing she was sure of was they were all going to hell bubbled to the surface.

Her stomach ached: too much coffee, and not enough food. She reached into her drawer for the ginger chews she kept at hand. She unwrapped one and popped it into her mouth to quell her stomachache and glanced at the clock on the computer screen. It would be at least forty-five minutes before Sally was back with their food.

Her phone vibrated with a message. The glowing red notification sent a rill of excitement down her spine. Maybe a quick fuck would be the ticket to a good night's sleep. A glorious, no-real-names hotel-room sex fest would be delightful. She thumbed open the Hit Me Up app and opened the message.

Disappointment washed over her. The message was from her most recent date. A bold butch who had given Eun several mind-bending orgasms that had made her strongly reconsider her self-imposed no-more-than-one-date rule. Until she stalked the woman on social media and found out she was not single as her profile claimed. Eun detested cheaters. She deleted the woman's message without reading it and tossed her phone onto her desk.

*

Morgan Wright parked her truck behind her sister's police cruiser. She tugged on her fluorescent yellow windbreaker with Wright's Lock Shop emblazoned on the back and grabbed her tool bag from the floorboard.

A sharp wind rustled the yellow-and-white daffodils along the side of the driveway.

"Hey." Miesha called from the yard. "Thanks for coming out on a Sunday."

Morgan slipped the tool bag strap over her shoulder. "What we got?" She surveyed the mid-century low ranch-style houses and manicured lawns lining both sides of the street.

"A neighbor called. No one's seen Mr. Park since Friday evening. The neighbor called after she knocked on his door and got no answer. Said his dog sounded like he was going to take her leg off."

Morgan frowned. She hated wellness checks. More often than not they were nothing, and then it took forever to get reimbursed from the police department for her time.

She nodded toward the security system sign. "Did you call them?"

Her sister barked out a laugh. "It's one of those fake signs. Like half of them."

Morgan rolled her eyes. A wooden post displayed a carved green-and-white sign proclaiming James Park, Esquire in gold script. A wide sidewalk split off into two and led to a second door on the front of the house.

"He works out of his home?"

Miesha flipped her notebook closed and tucked it in her shirt pocket. "He does. And his car is in the garage."

Morgan walked to the front door. A large brass deadbolt secured it. It was dusty and small cobwebs lined the frame next to the hinge. She opened the lid to the mailbox and a tiny spider scuttled away from the light. "Let's try the side door. Doesn't seem like this one is used much."

Morgan followed the curving walk leading to the side of the house. A low porch with an iron railing was sheltered by a red-and-white striped awning. As soon as she set foot on the porch vicious barking rang out.

Morgan glanced over her shoulder at her sister. "You better call Animal Control too." A trickle of sweat ran down her back.

"The department takes their calls on Sunday, so I'm Animal Control today. Will you hurry up? I don't have a good feeling about this." Miesha shifted her feet and rested her hands on her duty belt.

Morgan studied the locking mechanism. "For fuck's sake, you could have done this. You didn't need me. There isn't even a deadbolt." She drew a flexible metal shim from her tool bag and slid it between the door latch and the jamb. The barking on the other side grew frenzied. Morgan wiggled the thin strip of metal until the lock popped open. She twisted the knob in her hand. "Get ready, I think Cujo's on the other side."

Miesha stepped close. "Shove it open and then step behind me."

Morgan shoved the door wide and dropped behind her sister. A brown-and-white ball of fur and teeth flew at them. Morgan turned away and raised her hands over her face. The dog barreled past them into the yard. Morgan turned around to keep the animal in her line of sight. The dog stopped, urinated, and then bolted back into the house.

Miesha had disappeared inside the house. The small hairs on the back of Morgan's neck stood up at the silence. She hesitated. It wasn't in her job description to do more than open the door, but the lure of the dog and her own curiosity drove her steps and she entered the home.

The rank scent of urine and feces stung her nose as she walked through the door. In the middle of the kitchen floor, a man she assumed was Mr. Park lay stretched out facedown. A small pile of dog toys was scattered near him. The dog, a classically colored tan-and-white corgi so much smaller than his bark, lay with his muzzle on the back of the man's outstretched hand. His wary eyes settled on Miesha and Morgan.

"Easy, Cujo." Miesha knelt and reached down to check the man's neck for a pulse, more out of habit than any real hope of finding one because it was very apparent James Park, Esquire was dead. Morgan rubbed the back of her neck.

"Damn it." Miesha sighed as she rose to her feet.

"You know him?" Morgan rested her hand on her sister's shoulder.

"Met him a couple of times in court. Decent man. Good attorney. Fuck, I hate this."

The dog whined. Morgan inclined her head toward him. "What about him?"

Miesha shrugged. "I'll call the shelter. It's Sunday. I hope they answer."

Morgan knelt down and held out her hand palm up to the dog. "You saw it all, didn't you, buddy?"

The crackle of Miesha's radio became background noise as she called for the coroner and talked to her dispatcher. Morgan dared to lift her hand to stroke the soft fur. The dog leaned into her touch. She turned his collar so she could read his tag. "Rudy" was etched in the brass plate followed by a phone number. "Well, Rudy, it's nice to meet you."

At the mention of his name the dog lifted his head. His deep-brown eyes locked with Morgan's and he nuzzled her hand.

Miesha leaned against the counter. "Great. The coroner is out on another case. I'm going to be here a while."

"What if I took him?" Morgan raised her gaze to her sister.

"What?"

"Unless Mister Park's people are close. I'll take him. Only overnight. Until the shelter opens."

Miesha eyed her sister. "Isn't that how you got Beau? A lockout and eviction? And an 'oh I'll just keep him until the shelter opens'?"

"Well yeah. But..."

"But nothing. It's fine with me. On the condition you go get me coffee. I've got to stay here with Mister Park until Doctor Silvestri gets here."

"Done." Morgan stood up. "Come on, Rudy. Where's your leash?"

"You already named him?"

"No. It was on his tag." Morgan looked around the kitchen. Next to the back door was a hook and a bright-blue leash. She removed it and knelt down. She patted her leg. "Come on, Rudy. Want to go for a ride?"

Rudy stood and took a step toward Morgan. She sat back on her heels to wait. He waddled over to her and sat down. She hooked the leash on to his collar. He looked over his shoulder at Mr. Park. Morgan bit her lip. She gave him slack on the lead. Rudy walked over to Mr. Park, licked his cheek, and then walked toward the door.

Morgan shouldered her tool bag. "You want your usual?"

"Yeah. I'll be here. Leave the door open." Her sister turned and opened the kitchen window. "Maybe the cross-breeze will help."

Rudy scratched at the screen door. Morgan pushed it open and followed him out to the yard. He nosed about for a minute and then trotted forward.

He watered the azalea bush on his way down the sidewalk. A tall woman in a floral dress waved Morgan down. "I'm Mrs. Dunn, I called." She flapped her hand at the police car. "Where are they? Who are you? Where are you taking Rudy?" Morgan opened her mouth to speak but the woman ranted on. "Oh, my word. Something's happened. I should've called sooner."

Morgan lifted her cap and resettled it. "The police are inside. I'm sorry, I can't tell you anything."

Her eyes widened. "He's dead. I knew it. I know things." She crossed herself.

"I'm sorry, ma'am, I have to go." Morgan walked Rudy to her truck and opened the door.

He cast a baleful glance at her over his shoulder and rested his front feet on the running board. Morgan rolled her eyes at his expression before she picked him up and put him into the truck. He made three circles on the cushion and then settled into the passenger seat. Morgan cruised to the doughnut shop drive-through and picked up coffee for her sister and an empty cup. She poured water from her water bottle into the cup. "Hey, want some water?"

Rudy sat up and sniffed at the cup before he lapped at it. Cold water splashed over Morgan's hand and she held the cup as he drank. After he emptied the cup, Rudy lay down with his back to her.

On the drive back to Mr. Park's house Morgan reached out to stroke Rudy's fur. He huffed and shifted away from her touch.

"I get it buddy. I'm rushing you." Morgan left Rudy in the truck while she delivered her sister's coffee.

Miesha was standing on the side porch when Morgan returned. She took the cup Morgan offered.

"Thanks." She pursed her lips. "I've got to call his daughter, Eunice Park. She's listed as next of kin, so don't get too attached to Cujo."

"His name's Rudy, and I know." Morgan called over her shoulder as she strode back to her truck. Rudy barked sharply when she opened the door. "I wasn't gone that long."

Rudy huffed and lay down with his head between his paws. His tiny snores made Morgan smile on the ride home, and then sober as the circumstances of her newest rescue hit her. "You're gonna be okay, boy. I think. I hope."

Morgan drove through the sunny afternoon, wondering about the woman whose world was about to be upended at the news of her father's passing.

Chapter Two

"Do you need me to come over after I put Julie to bed? Jeff would be fine with it. We haven't had a good wine and bitch session in a while." Roslyn Cena's voice dropped to a whisper. "And believe me, I'm overdue.

"No. I'm good. I'm going to have an early evening. It will be a duck and cover day tomorrow. Heather will be on a tear." Eun tucked her legs up under her on the couch and settled back with her wineglass.

"You're sure?"

"I'm sure. See you next weekend?"

"See you then." Roslyn disconnected the call.

Eun pursed her lips as she considered calling Roslyn back. An evening with her best friend might be the thing to lift her funk. But facing down the senior partner of her firm with a hangover would be horrific. She replayed the last few minutes in the courtroom and the reading of the verdict in her thoughts. This wasn't the first case she had lost, but it was the first in a very long time. Eun had trusted Lew to do his job. How many times had she pushed aside the niggling buzz at the base of her skull? Ignored her gut feeling the case was too perfect? And now...And now the only thing that was going to help was large amounts of red wine, chocolate, and the sweet seduction of Cate Blanchett in *Carol* on loop.

She pressed play and tugged her weighted blanket from the back of the couch and settled it over her legs. She plucked the rose-and-gold paper from a square of Dolfin chocolate and popped it into her mouth. The soothing flavor of the perfect blend of cocoa and sugar spread over her taste buds. She lifted her wineglass to her lips and sipped. The tart Syrah blended perfectly with the lingering taste of chocolate.

Eun picked up her phone and opened the Hit Me Up app. After ten minutes of mindless scrolling, she placed her phone facedown on the coffee table unable to summon the strength to go through the dance of online flirting on the off chance she might find what she was looking for. Too closeted to date women in college, she'd been too busy in law school. And now she was what? Too jaded. Too many disastrous first dates and two ridiculous short relationships had her convinced she was better off with one-night stands and anonymous meet-ups for sex.

On screen, Cate was making eyes at Rooney Mara over the train set. Eun tugged the blanket up higher wondering if she'd ever find someone who looked at her the same way. A loud knock at the door made her squeak and spill her wine. Eun set her wineglass on the side table. She snatched a tissue from the box on the end table and dabbed her sweatshirt. Another knock, more insistent than the first, rattled the door. She struggled out from under the heavy blanket and bumped her shin on the coffee table.

"Hold on," she shouted at the door. Eun paused the movie as she pushed her feet into her slippers. In three long strides she was at the door. She turned the deadbolt and snatched the door open.

Two uniformed police officers stood on the doormat in the dim light of the hallway. The taller one's bright silver nameplate read Burgess. The second officer hung back, flanking the lead officer.

Officer Burgess inclined her head. "Are you Eunice Park?"

Eunice crossed her arms over her chest. "Yes."

"I'm Officer Burgess. This is Officer Malone. May we come in?"

"Depends."

Officer Burgess frowned. "On what?

"Why are you here? Do you have a warrant?"

A snorting sound from the other officer drew a sharp glare from Officer Burgess.

Officer Burgess pressed her lips in a thin line before she responded. "Ma'am, we are here on behalf of the Sikesville Police Department and have some information for you. About your father." Officer Burgess looked down at the floor before she brought her gaze back and met Eun's. The other officer stared at the ceiling avoiding Eun's eyes. "I think it would be better if we came in."

Eunice's pulse pounded in her ears and a sour taste rose in her mouth. "Yes." She backed up into the apartment. "Yes. Of course."

The police officer stepped in and closed the door behind her. "Are you alone, ma'am?"

"Yes. Please tell me." Eun dug her fingernails into her palms, the sharp pain focusing her, and she swallowed on a dry throat.

"Maybe we should sit down."

Eun straightened and squared her shoulders. "Tell me now. I assure you I am alone. I don't want to sit. I want you to stop wasting my time and tell me whatever you have to tell me."

Office Burgess grimaced. "There's no easy way to say this. Your father died. I'm sorry."

"What?" The sensation of her vision narrowing closed over Eun, and she swayed. "What? How?"

Officer Malone closed her hand around Eun's elbow to steady her. "Let's sit." She guided Eun to the couch and helped her to the cushion. She remained standing next to Eun.

"Saturday by the coroner's estimate." Officer Burgess's gaze settled on Eun. "A neighbor called because she was concerned. An officer responded this afternoon. Your father was deceased when the officer arrived."

Eun scrubbed her face with her hands and grabbed handfuls of her hair. "No. No. How? I just talked to him." Tears hovered and she blinked them back.

"The autopsy results won't be back for a while."

A wave of nausea swept through her. "Was he murdered? What are you saying?" She struggled to focus on the officer's face and his words. "I don't understand."

"All unwitnessed deaths are autopsied unless it's clear the cause of death. I can't tell you anything else."

Eun stood up and paced. "He was healthy. I talked to him last week. He was fine."

Officer Burgess stood up. "Is there anyone who can come and stay with you? A family member? A friend?"

Eun hung her head. "I'm fine."

Officer Burgess frowned. "We have a team. They can come and stay with you, for a bit."

Eun raised her shoulders and let them fall. "No. Thank you. No."

The second officer held out a card and packet of information. "This is the contact information for the police department in Sikesville and our support team. They'll call you in a day or two to check in."

"We're sorry, ma'am, about your father." Officer Burgess inclined her head toward the door. "Please call the number on the card if you need anything." She led the way and they left, closing the door behind them quietly.

Eun twisted the knob to and set the deadbolt. She leaned back against the door. The chill of the steel made her shiver as she slid down it. The back of her shirt bunched up, the cold metal raw against her skin. She clasped her knees to her chest and rocked. Her throat burned. A shuddering sob shook her frame. Tears burned her eyes as she wept for what she'd lost and what could, now, never be.

Chapter Three

Eun folded her clothes precisely and placed them into her suitcase, not seeing anything in front of her. A million questions swirled through her thoughts. Guilt settled over her, thick and heavy on her shoulders. Eun took the box holding the keys to her father's house from her top drawer and placed it in the outside pocket of her suitcase. She worried her lip with her teeth, stopping only when she tasted blood. Her fingers trembled as she tried to compose a text to her firm. After starting five times and deleting everything Eun pressed the call button for her employer's number.

Heather picked up on the second ring. "What? And it better be good for you to disturb my Sunday."

Eun winced at Heather's tone. It answered her question about how far from her favor she had fallen with the loss on Friday. "I'm not going to be in the office for the next two weeks. And maybe the week after."

"Isn't it customary to ask for time off instead of telling me?" Heather's voice dropped to a lethal pitch. "I can arrange for you to have a permanent vacation after your disgraceful and ridiculous performance on Friday."

"My father..." A wave of disbelief swept Eun over the edge of despair.

"Out with it. I don't have time for this." Heather's knife-edged voice snapped Eun out of her silence.

"I need to go home. My father died."

"Oh. Well. All right. But I can only give you a week."

Eun took the phone away from her face for a moment and stared at the screen. How had she worked for such a woman? Someone who could not even summon the common courtesy to express her sorrow over Eun's loss?

"I might need longer."

"He's dead. And from what you've said in the past it's not like you were close. I'll need you back in two weeks at the latest. We're going to have to work extra hard to make our numbers for this year."

"Fine." Eun disconnected the call and tossed her phone on the bed. She knelt on the floor and plucked shoes from her closet. She cradled the pair of black pumps in her hands. Her face, distorted and teary, was reflected in their shiny surface. Two weeks. Fifteen years of working for Heather and all she could spare Eun was two weeks? Low-key anger filtered in, underpinning Eun's sadness.

She rose and placed the shoes into their covers before settling them into her suitcase. After tucking a black suit and dark-navy suit into her hanging clothes organizer she zipped it shut. Eun retrieved her cosmetic bag from her bathroom, avoiding her reflection in the wide vanity mirror. After she finished packing she closed her bag and placed it by the door.

Eun returned to the bathroom and showered. She dressed in her most comfortable jeans and took time to search for her favorite faded T-shirt. She pulled it on, the kitten-soft cotton soothing. Eun snagged a fleece pullover jacket from the closet on her way out of the door of her condominium.

Grateful she had only had a few sips of wine, she typed her dad's address into her phone's direction app, not trusting herself to remember the route. She probably shouldn't be driving but who else would? No one. The isolation of her life loomed large.

Her mother was not someone Eun turned to in times of crisis. Friends? None she could ask to drive her to Ohio. So many things to do. Tell the family. She sighed. Her Uncle Max. She only had to call him. He would take on the job of calling everyone after he berated Eun, once again, for being the worst daughter in the world and telling her he knew why she didn't have a husband.

Eun doubted he knew the real reason; she wasn't out to her family. Her dad insisted she remain closeted about her sexuality. And now there was no reason to tell anyone in her extended family. After the funeral, Eun would be free of them. No more stressful holidays, or family gatherings. Alone. She was alone. And she liked it that way. Most of the time. But tonight, as she drove into dark night, she wished there was someone she could rely on besides herself.

*

During the ride to Morgan's home Rudy had slept curled tightly in a ball. Morgan had reached out a time or two to stroke his back. *Don't get attached.* Yeah, like Morgan had ever met a dog she didn't like or want to keep. She pulled up behind the building that housed the Lock Shop and her home.

The truck rocked side to side as she drove over the parking lot. The small lot behind the building was in sore need of a new topping with crushed run and grading. *Next year. Maybe.* The soft glow of the late afternoon sun peeped through the trees and backlit the scruffy grass of the tree lawn.

After she parked the truck Morgan reached out her hand toward Rudy. "Come on. It's okay." He sat up and sniffed her hand before he turned around and, with his back to her, lay down on the seat. "You can't sleep here all night. Come on." Morgan picked up the hefty ball of fur and set him on the gravel at her feet. He blinked at her sleepily.

"Let's go." Morgan led him over to the lawn and let him sniff for a few minutes before she led him up the stairs to her apartment. She typed in the passcode and waited for the lock to disarm before she entered. Rudy followed behind her, the click of his nails loud on the linoleum entry. Morgan shrugged out of her jacket and hung it on the hook before she kneeled down and unfastened Rudy's leash. "Go ahead, check it out." She unlaced her boots and set them on the mat beside the door.

Rudy padded around the kitchen. Morgan stepped around him and opened the cabinets. She'd kept Beau's food and water bowls. A handmade pottery set with Year of the Dog symbols etched into the glaze. A Christmas gift from her family, she had been unable to give the set away after his death. She filled the water bowl and placed it on the floor. "I'll get you some dog food tomorrow. Tonight, it's rice and hamburger."

Rudy woofed softly and turned away from Morgan. He walked the length of the kitchen and out into the living room. Morgan set up her rice cooker, added rice and frozen peas to it, and switched it to on to cook. The sounds of Rudy's nails and movements as he explored Morgan's apartment filled the silence. She took two premade hamburger patties from the freezer and placed them in a skillet, turned the flame to low, and covered it with a lid.

Rudy continued to circle her home, sniffing at the corners, pausing every now and then for longer investigations. He made four loops of her apartment before returning to Morgan. He jumped up and put both paws on her leg.

"I know it's weird." She scratched his ears. "I'm sorry." He leaned into her touch for a moment and then drew away. He lay down on the rug by the sink.

Morgan washed her hands and finished cooking the meat. The rice cooker clicked off. She spooned peas and rice on to her plate and spread another spoonful of the mixture on a larger plate to cool. After placing a hamburger patty on top of her rice and peas, she broke up the second patty and scattered it over the rice and peas on the dish for Rudy.

She carried both plates to the living room with Rudy trotting after her. After placing the plates on the wide coffee table, she picked up the remote and switched on the television.

"You like Formula One?"

Morgan scrolled through her collection of recorded races, settling on the 2019 Italian Grand Prix. "This is one of my favorites. Biggest upset in years. And the team owner is smoking hot."

Rudy cocked his head at her words and Morgan laughed. She sat on the couch and Rudy jumped up next to her. He tried to step on the coffee table to get to the food. "No. That's not how we do this." Morgan placed his plate on the floor between the couch and the coffee table and Rudy left the couch to gobble at his food.

Morgan wondered how long it had been since he had eaten. The bowls of water and food in Mr. Park's kitchen had been empty. Morgan balanced her plate on her lap and forked her food into her mouth. Rudy leaped up beside her and made a move toward her plate. "Oh no." Morgan held him back with one hand. "You've had enough. You'll get sick." Rudy huffed at her, went to the far end of the couch, and lay down with his back to her. "You can pout all you want, but you're not getting my food."

Morgan grinned to herself as she looked over at Rudy. *Yeah. Don't get attached. Too late. Damn it. Maybe they'll let me foster him. Until the family gets here. Eunice Park. Will she want to keep him?* Her thoughts took a melancholy turn as she thought about how devastated she would be if she got a call her pop was gone. She muted the television and dug her phone out of her pocket before she scrolled to her parents' number and called them.

"Hey, girl, what's going on?"

At forty-two, her dad calling her girl made her smile. "Just got back from helping Miesha on a call. Did you know James Park? Attorney in town?"

"I think we did the locks on his home office when he moved his office from downtown. Neil helped me. Why?"

"He was gone when we got there."

"You okay?" Her dad's voice was soft.

"I guess. It's the first time for me." Morgan sat back on the couch and put her feet up on the coffee table. "It was weird."

Rudy sat up, yipped once, walked to Morgan, and lay down with his head on her thigh.

"Who's that?'

"Rudy. Mister Park's dog. The shelter's closed on Sunday. I took him so Miesha wouldn't have to worry about it."

"Uh huh. Right. Well, don't get attached."

"I know." Morgan sighed and rubbed Rudy's head. "I'm hoping they'll let me foster him until the family comes."

"Are you sure that's good for you?"

The weight and warmth of the dog against her leg was comforting. "It'll be fine. I know I can't keep him, but it's good to have him here. I didn't realize how much I missed Beau."

"Do you think the family will want him?"

"Don't know. I'm hoping they don't."

"Hey there, your father, the phone hog, didn't say it was you. You all right?" Her mother's voice was loud, and Morgan pulled the phone away from her ear.

"Yeah, Mom. Just wanted to talk to you."

Her mother was off and running then, talking about everything and nothing. Morgan sat back on the couch and absorbed it all, grateful she could still hear their voices, and feeling sorry for a woman she didn't know who would never hear her dad's voice again.

*

Unable to concentrate, Eun switched off the podcast she had attempted to listen to. The red taillights of the few cars in front of her lit the night. She checked the estimated time of arrival on the travel app. *After midnight, and where the hell am I going to stay? Fuck I need to find a place before I get there. Should have thought of that before I left. So used to Sally doing everything when I travel.*

She left the highway at the next exit and turned toward the blue sign announcing a gas station and lodging. She pulled the car into the brightly lit gas station.

Her stomach ached but her jaw clenched at the thought of food. She filled the car with gas and then parked forward in the row of spots outside the convenience store. Eun tapped the screen and called Sally. By the fifth ring a wave of despair tinged with guilt swept over Eun. She pulled the phone away from her ear, finger poised ready to disconnect the call.

"Eun? What's up?" Sally's sleep-tinged voice came through the phone.

"Sorry I woke you. It's not important." Eun jiggled her leg, her anxiety ramping up.

"Well, I'm awake now so tell me."

"I'm not going to be in the office this week and maybe next week."

"Did that bitch fire you? Because of Friday?" The hate in Sally's voice made Eun smile at her loyalty.

"No. Not yet. My dad—" Eun swallowed hard."—my father died."

"What? Oh no, honey, I'm so sorry. I'll take care of things, don't worry. What do you need me to do?"

Eun rested her head on her steering wheel and closed her eyes. "I don't even know yet."

"I'll come over. You shouldn't be alone."

"No. I'm not at home. I'm driving to his house."

"Oh, Eun. You're not talking and driving, are you? Why didn't you call me?"

Even the gentle chastisement Brent was too much for Eun and tears came in great shuddering sobs. "No. Sorry." She croaked into the phone.

"Oh honey. I'm sorry, I didn't mean to make you cry."

Eun couldn't respond. She clutched her phone and the connection to the one person who had expressed sympathy and understood why it was so hard.

"Where are you?"

"About to cross the Ohio line." Eun pulled two tissues from her travel pack.

"You sure there isn't anything I can do?"

"Can you book me a room? I think you had one set up for next weekend, can you see if I can switch it? Or add on." Eun shivered. Would she even want to stay in her childhood home? Would she be allowed to?

"Done. And you call me if you need anything else. I'll take care of things on this end. I'll find you a room for tonight and text you the information about the reservation."

"Thank you. For everything."

"Take care of yourself. And remember to eat."

"I will."

Sally disconnected the call. Eun scrubbed her hands over her face. Food. The last thing she wanted right now was food. She levered herself out of her seat and went inside. One bathroom stop, two bottles of water, and an energy drink later and she was on her way.

Chapter Four

"Sikesville Shelter, this is Sheryl, how can I help you?"

"Hey, Sheryl, it's Morgan." Morgan rolled the edge of her T-shirt in between her fingers. Rudy sat at her feet, looking up at her. He had spent the night curled up with his head under Morgan's bed.

"Please tell me you are not canceling your shift."

"No. I'll be there on Saturday. Did Miesha send over the report?"

"Not yet, what's up?" The sounds of dogs barking in the background grew louder. "Sorry, I'm back in the kennels."

"I went with her on a wellness check yesterday morning and it wasn't good. I have the dog."

"Oh, no, that's horrible. I mean about the wellness check."

"Is it okay if I foster him? I mean until the family gets here."

"Yeah, you're on our list. Give me his tag number so I can record it. And that helps a bunch, hon. We're full at the moment."

Morgan reached down and scratched Rudy's neck. She slid his collar around to read his tag. Rudy shifted on the couch as he slept. She squinted at the tiny type and recited the numbers to Sheryl.

"Got it."

Morgan stood and stretched. "Do I need to bring him in for a vet check?" Rudy woofed softly and walked away from Morgan.

"No. His rabies is current, right?"

"Yeah, according to the vet tag."

"I'll make a record of this and then we'll wait until the family is contacted to see what they want to do."

Morgan glanced at the clock on the stove. "Oh damn, I was supposed to open five minutes ago. Gotta go."

"See you Saturday."

Morgan disconnected the call and shoved her phone into her pocket. "Rudy! Come on, boy, we have to go to work." She walked back to the living room. Rudy was still asleep on the couch. "Come on, boy. You can sleep in the shop." She touched his shoulder. He lifted his head and blinked at her. After snapping the leash on his collar, Morgan stepped back. "Come on. We're late."

He stood up and stretched languorously before he slid belly first off the couch. Morgan rolled her eyes at the dog. "Get with it. Come on." Rudy looked up at her. She led him out of the door and down the stairs. As she put her key into the back door of the locksmith shop, she heard the phone ringing. She rolled the keys and unlocked the door, dragged Rudy inside, and snatched up the phone.

"Wright's Lock Shop. How can I help you?"

"By opening on time." Her dad rumbled through the phone.

Morgan pursed her lips. "You called to check to see if I opened on time? What the hell, Dad?"

"Mister Billings is coming by today, and I want everything perfect."

"Dad, didn't we talk about this? The place is perfect. And if he doesn't want to lend to us it's his problem."

"I'll be there by nine-thirty. And please keep your temper."

A tug on the leash brought her attention to Rudy. "Uh, Dad. I've got Rudy with me."

"Who?"

"The dog. The one I'm fostering."

"Why? Why is the dog in the shop? You don't know anything about him. What if he's aggressive with customers? Or barks? Or shits on the floor?"

"He's not like that, Dad. He's been nothing but easy to take care of. I'll take him upstairs if he's a problem."

The chimes on the front door jingled. Rudy barked. Morgan covered the receiver with her palm. "Shh, Rudy." She spoke into the phone. "Customer's here. I have to go, Dad." She hung up the phone not waiting for her father to respond.

"Good morning. How can I help you?" Rudy pressed against her leg behind the counter.

A tall dark-haired woman strode toward the counter. "I need three copies of this, please." She held out a single key.

"Do you want standard blanks?

"I'm sorry, what? I want keys." She eyed Morgan. "This is a lock shop, right?"

Morgan flushed. "Yes. And I was asking if you wanted standard looking keys, or if you wanted them to look different, or use a blank with a larger base." She waved toward the wall of blanks. "Some people like to use the large ones for folks with grip issues, like kids or older folks. Some like to use a unique shape to help with identifying keys for folks with vision issues."

The woman turned and surveyed the collection of key blanks. "Oh." She pursed her lips and studied the pegboard with key blanks in colorful designs and unique shapes. "And more expensive. No. Standard will be fine." Her cell phone pinged. She frowned and tapped out a response. "I'm in a hurry. Can you do this?"

Rudy placed both paws on the back of the counter and barked sharply.

The woman's face broke into a wide grin. "Is that a corgi? Oh my gosh, I love corgis." She leaned over the counter and spoke to Rudy. "Are you a good boy?" Rudy wagged his tail and barked again. "You think I should have a special design? Well, why not?" The woman turned away from Morgan and studied the key rack.

Morgan glanced down at Rudy, who looked up at her and wagged his tail.

"I'll take these." She placed three blanks on the countertop: a tape measure, an old-fashioned shaped key blank, and one covered in emojis. "What's his name?"

"Rudy." Morgan swept the key blanks into her palm and picked up the woman's key. "I'll only be a moment."

"Take your time. Rudy, are you the best boy?" The woman cooed at Rudy. He placed both paws on the back of the counter and rose up on his hind legs. The woman stroked his head.

Morgan walked to the back of the shop, shaking her head at the change in the woman's attitude as she listened to her babble at Rudy and his occasional sharp yips in response. *If he's able to distract customers and get them to upgrade, Dad will be all for having him in the shop.*

*

Eun parked in the driveway of her father's home. The officer who had offered to escort her parked her police cruiser behind her. Eun exited her car and clutched the door keys in her hands.

Officer Wright rested her hands on her equipment belt. "Do you want me to go first?"

Eun lifted her shoulders and squared them. "No. I can do it."

She walked ahead of the officer to the side door. The faded red-and-white awning over the back door was streaked with green mold. She shoved the key in the lock and opened the door. The familiar smells of home and under it the faint smell of disinfectant hit her full force as she stepped through the door. Her footsteps echoed in the room.

Office Wright stepped through the door behind her. "It's been locked but if you want me to walk through it I will."

Eun rubbed her forehead. "No. I know it's safe." She studied the counter and the tidy row of canisters arranged next to the coffee pot. "Can you tell me where? Where was he?"

Officer Wright gestured to the floor "He was here, ma'am. His dog was lying next to him."

Eun looked up and frowned. "Dog?"

"Yes, ma'am. He's being fostered right now."

"My father didn't have a dog." Eun's mind spun back to all the times she had asked for a pet growing up and was turned down by her father. *I don't need one more thing to take care of, Eun.* His voice haunted her, the unspoken part of his refusal, his upset over having to care for her, like she was a burden, like he would have been happy if her mother had taken Eun when she left them.

"Miss Park?" Office Wright's voice brought Eun back from her woolgathering.

"Sorry, what did you say?"

"The dog is being fostered. Do you want me to call them and have them bring the dog to you?"

A dog to care for on top of everything else.

"Do I have to decide now?"

"No, ma'am." Officer Wright held out a card. "Here's how to contact me if you have any questions, or if you need anything. The number for the shelter is on the back for when you want to talk to them about the fostering."

Eun took the card and placed it on the counter. "Thank you, officer, you've been more than kind."

"Miesha, and please, I meant what I said. If you need anything, call. We have a support team and they'll call to check in on you." She passed Eun another card and a packet of information. "They're good at what they do."

"Thank you." Eun wrapped her arms around herself. "I'm fine."

Miesha tilted her head and met Eun's eyes. "If you say so." She nodded toward the door. "If you're sure you don't want me to walk through with you, I'll be going." Miesha closed the door as she left.

Eun walked to the door. The faded brown wood was scuffed and scratched at the bottom. She frowned at the lack of a deadbolt. Eun set the chain lock in place, slid down the door, and leaned back against it. She stared at the two dog bowls on the brightly colored rag rug and the empty space that had been the last place her father had been alive. No tears, she'd cried them all out in the hotel room last night. Her eyes were dry and scratchy and she rubbed them with the heels of her hands.

Her gaze flitted around the room and then settled on a framed photo of her father and a chubby tan-and-white dog. Her father was looking down as the dog looked up. The devotion on his face as he gazed at the dog made Eun's chest hurt. Love. Her father had loved a dog. Maybe it was easier. Dogs didn't talk back. Obeyed, and best of all, they didn't embarrass you by being queer.

A knock at the door startled her. She crawled away from the door and leaped to her feet. Eun pressed her face against the door and looked out of the peephole. A woman with a low cut fade stood on the porch. Tall, with thick shoulders, she was dressed in jeans and a tan work shirt with an embroidered patch that read Wright's Lock Shop on one side and Morgan on the other. A sharp bark and scratching at the door made her step back. She snatched the door open. The chain brought it up short and she swore as she closed it to unlatch it and then opened the door. On the other side of the screen door, the woman held on to a leash attached to the collar of a fat brown-and-white corgi.

"What do you want?" Eun called through the door.

The woman frowned. "Um, sorry to bother you. I'm Morgan." She held up the dog's leash. "I have your dog. I mean your father's dog." Her eyes were a light golden brown.

Eun looked away from Morgan's face. "I told the officer I'd call when I was ready."

"I'm sorry. I didn't mean to disturb you. I just thought...I'm sorry. Um, okay, call the shelter when you want me to bring him to you. If you decide you want him." Morgan turned and tugged the leash. The dog scratched at the screen door again as he whined and barked.

Eun stepped back and closed the door. She paced in the kitchen. *No. I don't need a dog right now. Not at all.*

The soft murmur of Morgan's voice and the continued whining of the dog made her bite her lip. *I don't need this.*

Eun blew out a breath. And she'd been rude. So rude, and she didn't need to be. The kind expression on Morgan's face and the way she had been so earnest tugged at her heart. She'd forgotten what a small town could be like. She raced to the door and yanked it open. Morgan was lifting the struggling dog into her truck.

"Wait!" Eun bolted down the porch steps and ran toward the truck. Morgan turned toward her with the dog in her arms. "I'm sorry. I'm not at my best. I'm Eun Park." Eun held out her hand.

Morgan flashed her a smile and shook her hand, her grip firm and warm. "Nice to meet you." She turned so the dog was facing Eun. "This is Rudy."

Eun held her hand out palm up. Rudy sniffed her palm and then licked it. Eun giggled in spite of her sadness. "I don't know anything about dogs."

Morgan placed Rudy on the ground between them. "I'm happy to keep him until you get settled." She reached out and rested the tips of her fingers on Eun's arm. "I'm really sorry about your dad. I should have waited. But Miesha said you'd be here."

Eun frowned. "Who?"

"My sister, the police officer, who escorted you this morning. I assumed you'd want the dog as soon as possible."

"I didn't even know my dad had a dog until today." Eun huffed out a breath, pushing aside the memories of the times her uncle had told her what a bad daughter she was for abandoning her father.

Morgan's eyebrows rose. "Oh. Well, I'm happy to keep him for you. I'll let the shelter know." She bent down and picked up Rudy.

"Don't go." Eun pressed her lips together. "I mean...would you bring him inside for a bit?"

Morgan put the dog down. "Sure."

Eun took a step back and stumbled over the edge of the sidewalk. She cried out and found herself caught up in Morgan's strong arms. She latched on to her wide shoulders and stared into the warm depths of her eyes.

Morgan steadied her and stepped back, releasing her. "You okay?"

Eun smoothed her hair with her hands. "Yes. Thank you. I'm a bit of a klutz sometimes."

Morgan's gaze settled on Eun's face. "Don't talk bad about yourself." She gestured to the uneven sidewalk. "Anyone could trip over that."

Rudy's sharp bark drew their attention. He was sitting on the back porch. He barked again.

"We're being summoned." Morgan held out her arm. "Let me help you. Those shoes look like they're made for the office." She gestured at Eun's pumps.

"I think the word you're looking for is impractical." Eun closed her fingers around Morgan's forearm.

Rudy barked again.

"You're so impatient. Simmer down." Morgan called to the dog.

Eun laughed. "You think he understands?"

"Well, yeah." Morgan chuckled. "He's pretty headstrong, but he was an angel at the shop this morning."

"The shop?" Eun released Morgan's arm and stepped up on the porch and opened the door. Rudy entered, dragging his leash behind him.

"Wright's." She gestured to her shirt. "I'm a locksmith. It's a family business."

"I remember. It's the shop in the neighborhood by Beechwood Elementary School, right?"

"That's the one." Morgan rested her hands on her hips.

Rudy walked to his bowl. It was empty, and he tipped it over with his foot. Morgan picked it up and filled it with water from the tap. "Here you go, boy."

Eun studied the woman in front of her and the easy way she had about her, her confidence and bearing. She had stud written all over her and any other time Eun would have been trying to figure out how to ask her out, but right now she was satisfied to bask in Morgan's calm energy.

Morgan tucked her hands in her pockets. "Do you have any questions?"

Eun swept her hair back with both hands. "Of all the questions I have, right now, the one at the top of the list is where can I get a decent cup of coffee?"

Morgan mouth lifted up in a crooked smile. "If you're up for leaving here, we could go to Bella's."

"And my second question is would you be able to put a deadbolt on this door? "

"Sure thing. We can stop by the shop so you can pick out the style you want."

Rudy scratched at a cabinet until he hooked it open with his paw. He latched his jaws around a bag of dog food and pulled it out of the closet. Kibble spilled over the floor and a few landed in his water bowl.

"Rudy!" Morgan picked up the bag from the floor and filled his bowl. She kneeled and plucked the wet kibble out of the water. Eun kneeled next to her and picked up the few kibble Rudy had missed as he gobbled up his food.

Eun stood and dropped the kibble in her hands into Rudy's bowl. After locating the dish soap in the cabinet under the sink, she washed her hands. The sounds of Rudy wolfing his food made her grimace.

Morgan rose to her feet and the soggy kibble dripped through her cupped hands. "I'll toss this out for the crows."

The door hinges squeaked when Morgan stepped outside. Rudy lifted his head and bolted for the door. "Hey, she's coming back."

Rudy barked and scratched at door, desperate in his attempt to leave.

Morgan opened the door and pushed him back inside by his chest. "I'm back. Easy." Rudy pushed himself into her arms and licked her face.

Stung by the dog's rejection, Eun turned away from the scene as she dried her hands. "Well, that settles it. Would you keep him for me?"

"He needs to get used to you." Morgan leashed Rudy. "Come on, let's get some coffee—I mean if you still want to."

"I want to, if you have the time." Eun picked up her purse and slung the strap over her shoulder. "Nothing for me to do here."

"I've got time. You want to take my truck? Or follow me?"

Eun rubbed her eyes. "I drove over from Chicago last night. Would you mind driving?"

"Happy to." Morgan led Rudy away to the truck.

Eun closed the door, the familiar sound of it stirring harsh memories of the last time she had left her father's house. She blew out a breath and squared her shoulders. Nothing for her here. Not now. Maybe there had never been. A stiff spring breeze stirred the blood-red tulips next to the porch and she pulled her jacket tighter against the chill. Morgan stood next to a large black pickup truck, a half smile on her face as she held the passenger side door open for Eun. Maybe there was something for her here after all.

*

The coffee shop was crowded. A woman dressed in yoga gear pushed past Eun to join a large group of women at a long table. Eun pressed closer to Morgan, the noise and crowd ratcheting up her anxiety.

"What'll you have?" the barista asked.

"The medium roast, please, black."

"Name?"

"Park." Eun moved ahead in the line and Morgan stepped up.

The woman behind the counter broke into a broad grin. "Your usual?"

"Yep, plus a doggo cup."

"You got a new dog?"

"Just fostering."

The woman wrote Morgan's name on the cup and pushed it toward the other woman working the counter.

They waited to pick up their coffee.

"You don't use Eunice?" Morgan nodded toward the cup with Eun's last name on it.

"No." She picked up Morgan's cup and the small paper cup next to it and passed it to her. "It's not my name. I use it because it's easier than listening to folks mangling my real name."

"What is your real name? If you're comfortable telling me." Morgan held Eun's gaze.

"Eun." Eun spoke slowly.

"Eun." Morgan took her time and repeated her name, clearly doing her best to copy her pronunciation.

"Eun. You kind of have to lean into it. Don't think of it as Eunice shortened. Leave off the u sound or think of it as a shortened u, like in the prefix 'un'. Close your eyes and listen."

Morgan's eyelids fluttered closed. Eun took advantage of Morgan's closeness to study her face, appreciative of her willingness to learn, and the sensual curve of her lips. She leaned in and spoke her name into Morgan's ear slowly.

Morgan opened her eyes and her gaze focused on Eun's face. Their eyes met and the coffee shop melted away as Eun stared into her gold-flecked brown eyes.

Morgan huffed out a breath and shifted her gaze away from Eun's face, breaking their connection. "Okay. How is this? Eun."

Eun took a step back and lifted her coffee in salute. "Good. And thank you. It's nice to hear it said correctly." She tilted her head toward the crowded shop. "Is it okay if we sit outside?"

"Sure. It'd be better for Rudy too."

They walked outside to two tables perched on the edge of the sidewalk.

"Let me get him." Morgan placed her cup and Rudy's cup on one of the tables before she trotted down the sidewalk to her truck.

Eun sat down and tucked her hands under her thighs to stop their tremble. Morgan's face was familiar and yet Eun couldn't place her. They were about the same age. With only one high school in Sikesville they more than likely had gone to school together.

Eun bit her lip. High school was a blurry memory. Focused on winning a scholarship, she had spent every waking moment studying to please her father. Rudy strode ahead of Morgan on the sidewalk. Eun took a sip of her coffee and studied them as they approached. Morgan's easy gait and self-confidence was a beacon, her stud strut so enticing Eun lost herself in staring at her.

Morgan looped the leash over the arm of her chair and secured Rudy. He sat down at her feet and she placed the small cup of water in front of him. He sniffed it before he drank.

Morgan lifted her cup and sipped. "Does this qualify as decent coffee?"

"It does. There wasn't anything like this when I lived here."

"The chamber of commerce has done a lot to bring in small businesses."

Eun glanced down the street at the store fronts. "I don't even recognize half the places. I used to love the food at Pop Li's. What's the new restaurant like?"

"Did you go to high school with Mai?"

Eun nodded. "I was in Yvonne's class. We went to college and law school together. I lost touch with her after graduation. What year were you?" She dabbed her mouth with her napkin.

Morgan lowered her chin to her chest. "I was supposed to be your year. But I missed so much school my sophomore year they held me back. I graduated the year after."

Eun chewed her lip as their conversation dried up. Embarrassed she had no memory of going to school with Morgan, she leaned down and scratched behind Rudy's ears to avoid her gaze.

"Mai moved back to town last year. Renovated the restaurant. It's great food. Hawaiian-style Asian fusion with local ingredients. She kept a few of the old dishes on the menu too. Yvonne moved back this summer." Morgan gestured to the top of the building. "They renovated the old apartments, made them accessible for Yvonne."

"I can't imagine moving back." Eun gazed at the building across the street.

"It's changed a lot." Morgan shifted in her seat. "Lot of new people and businesses." Rudy moved away from Eun, positioning himself under Morgan's chair. Eun sat back in her chair and drew her hands into her lap.

"He'll come around. It's not unusual for dogs who've lost their owners to latch on to the first person they spend time with after."

"I've never had a pet."

"Never?" Morgan placed her cup on the table and bent to rub Rudy behind his ears.

"No."

Morgan straightened and stopped petting Rudy, only to have him lean against her leg and raise a paw to her lap. She scratched him again. "Why? You like animals, don't you?"

"Yes. Well, in the abstract. I've never really had time to have a pet."

"Even as a kid?"

"No. My father said it was too much for him to have another thing to care about."

Morgan frowned. "Wow. No wonder you were shocked about the dog."

Eun looked away from Morgan's face. "I need to talk about something else. Tell me about yourself." Eun folded her hands on top of the table.

"Right. Sorry." Morgan leaned closer and touched the back of Eun's hand.

"Do you want me to install the deadbolt today? We could go to the shop after this."

"I don't want to disrupt your schedule."

Morgan grimaced and looked away. "I cleared my schedule for a meeting, but it was canceled at the last minute."

"Sorry."

Morgan turned back to Eun. "It's okay because I wouldn't have had the time to do this, with you."

The warmth in Morgan's eyes flowed over Eun and she sat up straighter in her chair.

"Well, I'm sorry about your meeting, but I'm not sorry to meet you." She inclined her head toward Rudy. "Or Rudy. Are you sure you're okay keeping him?"

"I'm happy to keep him as long as you want me to. Call the shelter and let them know we've talked about it."

Eun pursed her lips. "This is so weird. I need to find a funeral home for my dad's funeral arrangements. Do you have a recommendation?"

Morgan nodded. "McKnight's has always done a good job for my family."

Eun sighed and leaned back in her chair. "I feel like I should be more wrecked. I'm numb."

Rudy wandered around under their chairs tangling his leash in the chair legs until he couldn't move. He barked, the table amplifying the sound.

"You silly thing." Morgan unwrapped Rudy's leash. She stood and held Eun's gaze. "It's okay to feel any kinda way you feel. You want to walk a bit?"

Eun drained her coffee and tossed the cup in the trash. "Yes." She shoved her hands in her pockets. "And thank you."

"For what?" Morgan lifted her eyebrow.

"Being kind. Not judging me." Eun inclined her head toward the dog. "Taking such good care of something my father loved."

Chapter Five

They walked along Main Street. Morgan stole glances at Eun from under her lashes. Her dark hair was pulled back in a low ponytail at the back of her neck and the angles of her cheekbones stood out in sharp relief. Dark circles colored the skin beneath her eyes, stark against her skin. They walked in silence.

And Morgan relaxed into it. Right now, Eun Park seemed to need nothing more than her company. Morgan bit back the many questions she wanted to ask. Was she partnered? Did she have someone she would talk to about this? Would she ever want to talk to Morgan? Everything about Eun Park intrigued Morgan. She was an enigma, a puzzle. And Morgan lived to solve puzzles.

"You want to get something to eat? Ohana's, Mai's restaurant, will be open soon." Morgan nodded toward Rudy. "If you want, I could drop him off at my apartment and then we could go." Morgan fiddled with Rudy's leash.

"Um. I have…"

Morgan spoke over Eun, not wanting to hear the excuse she was trying to come up with.

"It's fine if you don't. I have some things I could do at the shop. If you come with me to pick out the lock and if you're going to be at your dad's house later, I could install it this afternoon. It won't take long."

Eunice tucked a loose strand of her hair behind her ear. "I'd like to have lunch with you but I have to make some calls." She bit her lip.

"I wish I could help you." Morgan stopped on the sidewalk. "What if I drop you at your hotel, drop Rudy off, and then come back to get you for lunch?"

"That works."

"Excellent."

"Give me your number. I'll text you when I'm on the way. Where're you staying?"

"Red Squirrel Inn." Eun dug in her purse and pulled her phone out. "Number?" They traded numbers on the street before they turned back toward Morgan's truck with Rudy walking between them. A giddiness settled over her, a ridiculous happiness over spending even a few more minutes with Eun. *Don't get attached. Don't think it's anything. She's only here to settle the estate. Nothing more.* But for a few moments Morgan let herself pretend it could be.

*

The hotel room was blissfully quiet after the cacophony of the coffee shop. Eun sat down on the bed and flopped back onto the pillow-top mattress. She mentally reviewed her morning with Morgan. *Why do I meet a woman so interesting when I'm so sad and stressed out? This is worse than when Mom left. At least Mom is still alive.* She dragged a pillow over and hugged it to her chest. *No sense putting off the calls any longer.* She pulled her phone from her bag and pressed the number for her Uncle Max's phone. On the fifth ring her uncle picked up.

"*Yeoboseyo.* Hello?"

"Hello, Uncle Max."

"Why are you calling?"

"My father's dead."

"What? What? When?" her uncle shouted.

"Saturday."

"My brother's been dead for days and you're calling me now? What kind of niece are you?" Eun held the phone away from her ear as her uncle went on, switching between Korean and English.

She waited for him to take a breath and blurted. "I only found out myself on Sunday. I got here late last night."

"I cannot believe you, Eun."

"I'm sorry." Eun smoothed her hand over the bedspread.

"I'll be there tomorrow. When is the service? Have you even made any plans?"

"I've been waiting for the body to be released. I'm talking to McKnight's funeral home after I get off the phone with you."

"You need to wait. You've never done this before. I know what has to be done."

"No. I've got this. I'll let you know what the plans are."

"You think this is all your decision? I'm his brother!" Her uncle screeched into the phone.

Eun sat up and tossed the pillow across the room. "And I'm his daughter and since I'm paying for it, it's my call. Unless you want to foot the bill, you will stay out of it." She disconnected the call while her uncle was still speaking. One down. Now the other call she dreaded to make.

She dialed her mom's number.

"Hello! A peaceful day to you and how may I help you today?"

Eun grit her teeth. "Hello, Mother."

"Eun, how marvelous to hear from you. Are you okay?"

"No. No, I'm not. I don't know how to say this. Dad died."

"Oh no. I thought I felt a disturbance in the universe. I knew something must be wrong."

Eun rolled her eyes. "Okay. Well, I wanted to let you know."

"I'll come right away. I'm sure your chakras are out of balance. I didn't like being married to your father, but I got you out of it so there is that."

"No. I'm only going to be here long enough to do the funeral thing and then I have to get back to work."

"What? You can't be serious. You loved your dad—he loved you, even if he had a hard time showing you." Her mother's voice was soft and genuine. Gone was the syrupy tone she used with her clients.

"I know." Eun pinched the bridge of her nose as a headache bloomed behind her eyes. "I know that. But he's gone. All I want to do is get this part over with so I can get back to the only thing that makes sense in my life."

"I'm coming there. You can't face that crew alone."

"You make it sound like war."

"Sweetie, I was married into that bunch long enough to know how they're going to be. You need my support."

"You don't have to do this."

"I do. I wasn't there when you were growing up. I can be there for this. Let me?"

Eun swallowed on a dry throat. "Thanks. I could use some help with Uncle Max."

"Let me know the arrangements and I'll be there." Her mom disconnected the call. Eun fell back on the bed, exhausted by the phone calls and what she still had left to do. She summoned her last bit of strength and called the funeral home to make an appointment to come by and discuss the options for her father's funeral.

She glanced at the bedside clock's red glowing numbers. She needed to sleep. But first food. And Morgan. Eun rolled off the bed. In the bathroom she splashed cold water on her face before she brushed her teeth. Her phone vibrated and excitement skittered down her back as she read Morgan's text.

Chapter Six

Morgan opened the door to her apartment and led Rudy inside. "All right. I'm going to be gone for a bit. Be good." Rudy's doleful gaze settled on Morgan's face. "Nope. Not falling for it. You'll be fine." She sat down on the sofa and patted her lap. Rudy leaped up and lay in her lap. She stroked his fur and rubbed his ear. "You're going to be fine and I'll be back soon." Morgan eased him off her lap. He made three circles and lay down on top of the folded blanket she had placed on the end of the couch.

Morgan took a few minutes in the bathroom to wash her face. She lifted her shirt and sniffed. *Okay. Why am I worrying about my shirt? This is not a date. This is lunch. Just lunch. Chill, Morgan.* She closed the door behind her and trotted down the steps. She stopped off at the lock shop. "Hey, Pop. What's up?"

"Nothing. Made an appointment for you tomorrow. New locks on a duplex on Maple."

"We get those new digital deadbolts in?"

"In the back. I haven't added them to the inventory."

She walked around the counter to the back storage room. She opened the carton and pulled out a box with the new deadbolt. "These are slick." She carried it out to the front counter. "I'm taking this one."

"For where?" Her dad scratched his beard. "I didn't have anything for you on the schedule. I still can't believe that asshat canceled at the last minute."

"Well, we don't want to borrow enough. I bet if we wanted to borrow four hundred thousand dollars his ass would have been here."

Charles Wright glanced at the ceiling. "I reckon the roof will hold another year if we don't get the loan."

Morgan chewed her lip. "I hate to borrow anything. Maybe I can work something out with the roofer."

Her dad sighed. "If business doesn't pick up, we won't even have to worry about the roof."

"It's going to be okay. We've been through tough times before."

Her father raised an eyebrow. "Not like this."

Morgan placed the lock on the counter and wrapped her arm around her dad's shoulders and hugged him. "We're Wrights. We don't quit. I have faith in us."

Her dad leaned his head against hers. "How did you get to be so smart?"

"Listening to you." She gave him a squeeze. "I'll be out the rest of the day. Call me if anything comes in."

"You still didn't say who the lock was for?" Her dad picked up the stub of pencil he kept roped to the schedule book.

"Park."

"The dead guy?"

"His daughter, who is most definitely alive."

"Behave yourself."

"I'm always professional, Pop."

"Uh huh. Call your mother later, she wants to talk about Sunday. Neil is bringing his girlfriend to dinner."

"Will do."

Morgan strode out of the shop and around the corner to her truck. Her father's warning to behave herself brought her up short and she slowed her pace. "It's not a date," Morgan repeated quietly to herself in the confines of her truck.

*

Morgan parked her truck along the shady street. She jiggled her leg as she texted Eun. A fat sparrow landed on the sidewalk and hopped along, stopping here and there to peck at the edges. She jumped when her phone vibrated with Eun's reply.

Out in a minute.

Morgan huffed out her relief. She had convinced herself on the drive over to the hotel that Eun would have changed her mind, that Morgan had pushed too hard and she was not interested in having lunch with her.

The door to the bed and breakfast opened. Eun stepped out onto the porch and looked up and down the street. Morgan climbed out of her truck, stood on the running board, and waved her arm.

Eun looked up, crossed the street, and walked toward the truck. Morgan hurried around and opened Eun's door for her. Eun eyed the truck as if taking it in for the first time. "This thing is so huge."

Morgan chuckled. "But it's a beast in the snow. I plow our lot and do the others to make a little extra." She held out her hand.

Eun clasped it and let Morgan assist her into the truck. She fastened her seatbelt and placed sunglasses over her eyes. "Thank you for waiting."

Morgan flushed. "It wasn't a big deal." She hurried to the driver's side and climbed into the seat. She passed the box containing the new lock to Eun. "This is our newest.

It's digital and you can reset the code remotely if you want to." She started the truck. "I don't know what you have planned for your dad's house, but this would make it easy if you were going to have realtors show it or if you wanted to rent it out."

Eun placed the box on the console between them. "I'm sure it's fine. I trust you."

"Why?" Morgan pulled the truck into the street.

Eun leaned back against the door. "The dog likes you. And you seem genuine. And kind. I've been an attorney for a long time. You get a sense of people. You have to trust your gut."

Morgan drove them toward the downtown area. "Why law? Did you always want to be a lawyer?"

Eun huffed out a breath. "My dad. It's not what I would have picked for myself."

Morgan chewed her lip. "I hear that." She turned on to Main Street and found a spot down the block from Mai's restaurant.

Eun waited for the traffic to clear before she exited the truck. "You didn't want to be a locksmith?"

Morgan shrugged. "I don't know what I wanted to do. This was an easy thing."

"And expected?" Eun walked around the truck to join Morgan on the sidewalk.

"Kinda. They thought my brother Neil would want to do it, but he's a nurse. Miesha made it clear from when she was in kindergarten, she wanted to be a police officer."

They entered the restaurant and passed the Seat Yourself sign and chose a booth midway down the dining area.

"Hey, Morgan, I'll be right there," the server called.

"Take your time, Noah." Morgan relaxed into the booth and rested her arm along the top. "I love their take on *Gyeran-jjim*. They make it with local duck eggs. It's over the top good. I like their classic Asian dishes best, but anything is good."

"My grandma would be proud of your pronunciation. And this place sure didn't look like this growing up. I miss the crazy blowfish hanging lanterns." Eun gestured toward the bar. "They have a liquor license? I thought the whole county was dry."

"Used to be. Other cities petitioned the state and they started granting liquor licenses. It was one of the things the city council changed, to bring in new restaurants and business. And weekend festivals in the summer. They are super popular. Did you see the wine and art place down the street? That place is booming on Saturdays."

The server placed two menus on the table. "Hey, Morgan. You're later than usual." He turned toward Eun. "Hi, I'm Noah and welcome to Ohana. Our special today is the spring roll pizza. I'll give you a few minutes to read over the menu."

Eun studied the menu. "They have a bit of everything from everywhere, don't they? Pop's had Korean-style fried chicken. Do they still do that? It was my favorite growing up."

Morgan smoothed her fingers over the menu card. "It's on the dinner menu. Mai said she wanted to make it so folks could find at least one thing they liked from when her parents ran it. She's added a bunch of new dishes too. Their spring roll pizza is amazing if you're in the mood for something more than the Gyeran-jjim, but it's like a meal the way they make it."

"You come here a lot, I gather?" Eun placed her menu on the table and leaned back against the booth.

"I'm not so much into cooking."

Eun unfolded her napkin and placed it in her lap. "Me either. I have every delivery place within five miles of my home on speed dial."

"No one cooks for you?" Morgan fiddled with the edge of her napkin.

"Not partnered if that's what you're asking." Eun tilted her head to the side. "You?"

"Nah. I'm single."

"An eligible woman like you?" A half smile played over her face.

Morgan barked out a laugh. "Yeah. Well, I don't think I'm all that."

Eun raised an eyebrow. "I bet some folks do."

Morgan let herself get lost in the bold appreciation in Eun's gaze.

"I could say the same." She focused on Eun's eyes. "It's hard for me to believe you're single."

Eun shrugged. "I've never wanted to settle down."

Morgan pursed her lips. "Never found the right guy?" She hoped like hell she had not made a wrong assumption.

"No. Never found the right woman." Eun peered into Morgan's face. "Are you surprised?"

"Nope. Just hoping." Morgan leaned back in the booth.

Eun mirrored her position and met her gaze.

They both startled when Noah placed two glasses of water on the table. "You ready to order?"

"I'm going to have the Gyeran-jjim, Noah."

"I'll have the Pad Thai, please."

"Got it. Anything to drink?"

"Water only, thank you."

"Me as well." Eun passed the menus to Noah.

Morgan leaned forward and rested her elbows on the table. "Your phone calls go okay?"

"As well as they could." Eun drummed her fingers on the tabletop. "My uncle's coming."

"I take it that's a bad thing?" Morgan unfolded her napkin and placed it on her lap.

Eun blew out a breath. "Yes. He hates me, hates my mom."

Morgan frowned. "Family drama is the worst. And why does he hate you?"

Eun spun the wide silver ring on her right hand. "I'm not what he thinks a daughter should be. He thinks I abandoned my father. That I'm ungrateful. Unnatural."

Morgan rested her chin in her hand. "That's a lot."

Eun raked her hair back with both hands. "I've faced down worse judges, it will be fine. I need to get through this."

"If you need anything please ask. I'm in control of my schedule most days."

Eun sat back in the booth. "That's very kind of you. At some point, I'll need a realtor."

Morgan knotted her hands together. "To sell the house, or rent it out?"

"Sell." Eun sipped her water.

"You've never thought about moving back here?"

"Not once. I'm not sure I could handle the lack of anonymity."

Morgan quirked her mouth. "Yeah, the 'everyone is in your business' stuff is hard sometimes."

Their meals arrived. Morgan lifted her spoon to break the fluffy egg covering the rich broth beneath.

Eun inhaled. "Smells divine."

Morgan pushed the bowl toward her. "Do you want a bite?"

Eun hesitated, her spoon poised over the bowl. "Are you sure?"

"Wouldn't offer if I didn't mean it." Morgan held Eun's gaze.

Eun spooned a bite of the egg custard into her mouth. Her eyes closed as she chewed slowly. She hummed her satisfaction when she swallowed. Eun opened her eyes, and her gaze seared Morgan with its boldness. "That is the best thing I've had in my mouth in a long time."

Morgan's mouth went dry watching Eun's face and then her elegant throat work as she ate. Her eyes locked on Morgan's face and she looked away from her intense gaze. The edge of the table pressed into her palm where she gripped it. Morgan scooted forward in the booth.

"So delicious. Do you want some of mine?" Eun slid the plate of Pad Thai closer to Morgan and tilted her head to the side.

"You sure?" Morgan picked up her fork and held it poised above the fragrant dish of noodles. A current of want crackled between them.

Morgan returned Eun's bold stare. "Very."

The sparkle in Eun's eyes and her wolfish grin sent a bolt of desire through Morgan.

Chapter Seven

"Let me get this." Eun reached for the bill jacket.

"No. That's not right. You've got a lot of expenses right now. Let me get it." Morgan rested her hand on the back of Eun's hand. "I asked you to lunch, let me get this. Please."

Eun released the bill folder. "Okay. And thank you."

Morgan smiled as she tucked the cash to pay for their lunch into the back folder. "My pleasure."

"I've been out with a few folks who think dating a lawyer is their golden ticket. I only dated other lawyers for a while, but it was so incredibly boring I gave up."

Morgan tilted her head to the side. "I get that. I've had a few folks treat me like I was a money machine." She shifted in her seat. "Is this a date?" She plucked at the shoulder of her work shirt. "I feel underdressed."

Eun quirked her mouth. "You tell me, you're the one who asked me to lunch. Is it?" She settled the strap of her purse over her shoulder and basked in Morgan's flirtatious energy. The intimacy building between them emboldened Eun. Morgan's delicious flirting was a pleasure she had not experienced in years. *Is she serious? I sure as hell am. Not been this thirsty in ages. She treats me like a queen and doesn't seem to want anything from me at all. I sure as hell want something from her. No, not something. Her. I want her. Think. How to do this?*

Morgan rubbed her thumb over the curves of the water glass. "I'd like it to be."

"But?"

Morgan frowned. "I know you're in a vulnerable place right now. I don't want—"

"To take advantage of me?" Eun lifted her shoulders and let them fall. "How noble. And I'm a grown woman, Morgan. Not a tender-hearted girl." She pinned Morgan in place with her gaze and lifted an eyebrow. "Although, your concern is touching."

Morgan leaned back in her chair. "What I wanted to say was if it was a date, I'd want to take you someplace as charming and elegant as you are."

Eun bit her lip and inhaled sharply. "Let's just leave it at 'not a date.'"

Morgan stood abruptly and pushed her chair under the table. "I'll pay this. Meet me outside?"

Eun nodded her agreement. She watched as Morgan walked away, her posture tight, gait stiff. "You blew it, Park." Eun spoke softly to herself as she left the table. She lifted her chin and walked out of the restaurant.

*

They walked along the street toward Morgan's truck. Eun slowed her pace as she searched for the words she wanted to ask Morgan to extend their "not date." *How do I ask for what I want? How do I tell her I want to take her back to the Red Squirrel, strip off her clothes, and lose myself in her light-brown eyes and delightful body?*

They arrived at the truck. Morgan rested her palm on the wide hood of the truck. "I can install the lock today if you want." Morgan tilted her head toward the sun hanging low in the sky. "It's not too late."

Eun stepped closer and rested her hand on Morgan's arm and squeezed it, enjoying the smooth curve of her forearm muscle under her palm. "Would you take me back to the inn before we pick up my car?"

Morgan leaned closer, the heat from her body filling the gap between them. "Sure."

Eun crossed to the passenger side and waited for Morgan to unlock the door. *Ten minutes. I have ten minutes to come up with a reason for her to come to my room. Direct. It's always best to be direct.*

They caught green lights all the way to the inn and were there in eight minutes. Eun gripped her purse strap tightly. She lifted her hand and smoothed her hair as the truck slowed to a halt and Morgan parked.

Morgan turned in her seat to face Eun. "I'll wait."

"No." Eun leaned across the console separating them and leaned close to Morgan. "No, I don't want you to wait."

Morgan shifted in her seat. "No? Oh, okay. Sorry I said what I said at lunch, I—"

Eun raised her finger and placed it across Morgan's lips to stop her apology. "Shh. Please don't apologize. Come to my room." She shifted her hand and cupped the back of Morgan's neck. "Please." She held her gaze a moment, searching for Morgan's consent in her eyes.

Morgan cupped Eun's elbow, her hand warm through Eun's blouse. She shifted in her seat and drew Eun closer, their mouths a breath away.

"I want—" Eun pressed a kiss to the corner of her mouth "—you. Will you come in?"

"Yes."

Eun moved her mouth to Morgan's lips. Soft and smooth and Eun wanted to devour her in the truck. She kissed her, tracing her tongue over the seam of her lips. Morgan opened to her kiss. Eun delved into her mouth, caressing with her tongue. Morgan's arm curled around her neck. Eun took the kiss deeper. Her nipples hardened. Her body ached for Morgan's touch. She broke the kiss and looked into Morgan's eyes and squeezed the back of her neck gently. "You're sure?"

"Yes." Morgan rubbed her palm over Eun's back in a slow circle. "And you?"

"Very." Eun kissed Morgan's cheek before she released the back of her neck. She picked up her handbag and slung the strap over her shoulder. She opened the door to the truck and slid out. Eun looked both ways before she crossed the street. A rill of pleasure shot through Eun when she heard Morgan's door close and her footsteps as she ran across the street. Morgan wrapped her arm around Eun's waist, and they walked toward the Red Squirrel together.

*

Morgan bolted from the truck and slammed her door shut. She caught up with Eun as she crossed the street. Morgan looped her arm round Eun's waist and pulled her close. Their hips brushed as they walked down the sidewalk to the inn and anticipation twisted inside Morgan's chest.

At the door, Eun keyed in the code before she pushed it open. Eun reached back and caught her hand. She laced their fingers together and pulled Morgan along behind her. At the stairs, she leaned in, pressed Morgan against the stairwell wall, and kissed her again. Hot and urgent and so delicious. Morgan groaned as Eun's hands gripped her hips. She held Morgan in place, and Morgan gave over to her vicious kiss. She plundered Morgan's mouth, taking what she wanted, what Morgan wanted to give. Morgan surrendered to her demanding kiss. Her clit hard and aching, she panted when Eun pulled back. Her eyes gleamed. She brushed a light kiss over Morgan's lips before she turned and led her up the stairs. The sway of Eun's hips under her light wool pants was a decadent temptation as she walked up the two flights of stairs to her room. Mesmerized, Morgan stared and wiped her damp palms on her jeans. On the landing, unable to stop herself, Morgan cupped Eun's ass with both hands and squeezed lightly, rewarded by Eun's quiet moan.

Eun opened the door to her room and they stepped inside. She spun and shoved Morgan up against the door. Fisting her hands in Morgan's shirt, she kissed her again. Morgan clutched Eun's hips and rocked against her as she trailed kisses down the side of Morgan's neck.

"So good," she whispered as she nibbled Morgan's earlobe while palming her breast with one hand. She flicked her thumb over Morgan's stiff nipple. Morgan trembled and a flood of desire soaked her briefs. Eun pulled her shirt loose from her pants and scratched her short nails over Morgan's skin, making her shiver.

Morgan rocked against Eun's hips, and she groaned against her neck.

Eun kissed and licked her collarbones, her lips soft and hungry.

"Take it, Eun, take what you want." Morgan spoke against the shell of Eun's ear before she nipped and sucked her earlobe. Eun raked the sharp edge of her teeth over Morgan's taut neck and then soothed the spot with her tongue. Morgan held on to her ass, holding her in place, and ground against her. Eun grabbed both sides of

Morgan's work shirt and yanked it hard. The sharp snick of all the snaps opening at once, and the cool air on Morgan's skin made her quiver. Eun shoved the shirt open and drew it over Morgan's shoulders.

She splayed her hands over Morgan's stomach and kissed the hollow between her collarbones. The backs of her knuckles brushed the skin of Morgan's belly when she unfastened her belt. Eun unbuttoned the top of Morgan's pants as she brought her lips close to her ear. "You are so handsome." She slid a finger into the top of Morgan's briefs and teased the tight damp curls above her clit. "So bold, telling me to take what I want. You like it this way. You like to be handled, don't you?" She whispered, the little puffs of her breath setting Morgan's skin afire.

"Push a little lower and you tell me." Morgan spoke against her skin.

Eun slid her finger over her slick curls. Morgan groaned and set her legs wide, pressing into Eun's touch.

"So wet." Eun teased her fingers over Morgan's aching clit. "I want you in my mouth."

Morgan moaned, bereft when Eun pulled her hand free and licked at the tips of her fingers. "More. Please."

"Bed." Eun shoved away from Morgan. She undid the three top buttons of her shirt before she pulled it over her head and tossed it to the floor. A white bra covered her thick brown nipples, pressed against the sheer fabric of the cups.

Eun toed off her shoes before she yanked the duvet off the bed. She held Morgan's gaze, and her mouth pulled into a feral smile as she unfastened her pants. The black fabric pooled at her feet, and she kicked free of them. With one hand she yanked the covers to the foot of the bed before she crawled to the middle of it and lay back. Pin-up perfection in panties and bra, Eun rolled to her side, leaned on her elbow, and rested her chin on her hand.

Morgan flushed, heat rising in her face under Eun's appraisal.

She crooked her finger at Morgan. "Come here."

Morgan crossed to the bed. She leaned down and kissed Eun.

"Get your clothes off. I want to see you." Eun scraped her nails over the back of Morgan's neck.

"Give me a minute." Morgan sat on the side of the bed to unlace her boots. Eun slid up behind her and cupped her breasts. She thumbed her nipples through the soft cotton of Morgan's workout top and nibbled at her neck.

Morgan huffed out a breath. "I'll never get these off if you keep doing that."

Eun nipped her neck. "Sassy, aren't you?"

"Practical. And didn't you say something about wanting to lick me?"

"Oh, yes." Eun dropped her hands lower and thrust them under the band of her briefs. She gripped Morgan's hipbones and stroked her fingers over the taut skin of her belly. "Is this distracting?"

Morgan finished unlacing her boot and toed it off. "Hell, yes."

Eun licked a line along her jaw and sucked on Morgan's earlobe. "How about this?"

Morgan laughed. "Damn it, Eun. I'm trying to get naked here."

Eun leaned back and traced her fingers down Morgan's spine and then withdrew her touch. "Fine. But hurry it up."

Morgan finished with her boots and then stood. She stripped off her bra and tossed it to the floor. In one movement, she shucked off her pants and briefs. The second she stepped out of her pants, she froze as Eun's gaze traveled to the keloid scars over her legs and then back to Morgan's face. "Car accident?"

"My sophomore year. It's why I didn't graduate with you." She held Eun's gaze, the frenzy of the moment slowed.

Eun frowned. "You okay?"

"I will be." Morgan flushed. "I haven't been naked with anyone I haven't told in a while. Usually I remember to say something."

Eun patted the bed and Morgan climbed in next to her. "We all have scars. Yours are on the outside." She planted a tender kiss on her cheek. Eun bent and traced her tongue along the soft curve of Morgan's breast before she closed her mouth over her nipple and sucked hard.

Morgan raised her hand and cupped the back of Eun's head. She tugged her ponytail gently. "Take your hair down? Please."

Eun sat up and gazed into Morgan's eyes. "You do it."

Morgan reached up and pulled the elastic holder from Eun's hair.

Eun sat on her heels and shook her hair out before she cupped Morgan's face and kissed her. She straddled Morgan, sprinkling kisses along her jaw, and then her neck before she kissed the wide valley between her small breasts.

Morgan wrapped her fingers in the silken strands of Eun's hair. With one hand she unclasped her bra. Eun's breasts spilled out of the cups. Bracing herself against Morgan, Eun shrugged out of her bra and tossed it aside before lowering herself to Morgan's body.

Morgan caught Eun's hard nipples in her fingertips, and she rolled them.

Eun gasped and arched into her touch, pressing more of her breasts into Morgan's hands. "Fuck, yes. Harder."

Morgan squeezed her nipples tightly. Eun rotated her hips in a slow grind, the alternating pressure and release on Morgan's clit a delicious tease.

Eun placed her hands over Morgan's where they cupped her breasts. She leaned down and kissed Morgan, her mouth, liquid seduction as she pulled Morgan's hands from her breasts and laced their fingers together. She raised Morgan's hands over her head. "Keep them there," she whispered. With a sinister glint in her eyes, Eun nodded toward the bedrail. "You might need to hold on."

Eun's soft command spun in the silky huskiness of her voice caught Morgan in its web, and she clasped the bottom of the headboard.

"Don't let go." Eun kneeled on the bed. She stared down at Morgan's body, her gaze burning as she smoothed her hands over Morgan's body. She palmed her breasts, squeezed them hard, and pressed them together. She licked the channel between them before she rolled Morgan's nipples into tight peaks. She sucked one and then then other, alternating in a maddeningly slow rhythm. Morgan's belly tightened. The ache in her clit built and she shifted her legs and rocked her hips, seeking contact. "Touch me. Please."

"Patience." Eun took her time kissing and nibbling Morgan's breasts, each kiss and nip a sweet torture as she held her body away from Morgan.

Need for release built in Morgan. Her hands ached where she gripped the headboard. She closed her eyes. "Please. I need. I can't—"

Eun stopped and rose over Morgan. She kissed her languidly, lingering on her lower lip. Morgan sighed into the kiss; the intensity of the moment faded. Eun rubbed her thumb over her cheek. "Look at me."

Morgan opened her eyes.

"If you need me to stop, say red, if you need me to slow down say yellow. Okay? Unless you want to stop?" Eun traced her nail over Morgan's cheek.

"No! Please don't stop." Morgan flushed, her ears burned, and she turned her face from Eun's gaze.

"Hey." Eun clasped her jaw and tugged. "Look at me, please."

Morgan turned to Eun.

"We can do this any way you want, Morgan. If you're not comfortable with this, it doesn't mean we can't have sex."

Morgan swallowed on a dry throat and moved her hands from the headboard. She looped her arms around Eun's neck. "I like what you're doing. I'm not used to not being the top."

A half smile lit Eun's face. "I'm the first to flip you? I'm honored." Eun leaned her brow on Morgan's forehead. "Let me finish you?" She feathered her fingers over Morgan's clit. "Please?" She kissed Morgan again. The room faded, and Morgan's world became Eun's mouth on her lips and her fingers between her legs.

Morgan spread her legs and moved her hands to the headboard. "Yes. Please."

"Spread your legs." Eun moved to kneel between Morgan's legs and rested her palms on Morgan's thighs.

Morgan opened her legs wide. Eun lowered her head and blew warm air over Morgan's damp tight curls before she fluttered her tongue over her clit.

Morgan moaned. "You're driving me crazy." She shifted her hands, tightening her grip on the headboard. "Finish me, please."

"You want me to suck you?" Eun drew a circle with her tongue on Morgan's thigh. Morgan shuddered and arched her hips up, seeking contact with Eun's mouth.

"You want to come in my mouth?"

"So much." Morgan thrashed her hips. "Don't make me wait."

"Lay still and trust me." Eun placed her hands on Morgan's thighs and held them down. "Let me do this."

Morgan panted and lowered her hips. The sensation of Eun taking control made her tremble, her body aflame with desire. Eun held her gaze as she teased the pad of her finger over one of Morgan's tight nipples. Her eyes focused on Morgan's face. "You're sure you're okay with this? I won't stop again unless you say 'red.'"

"Please don't stop. I'm okay. I trust you. Please don't stop." Morgan released the headboard and rubbed her thumb over Eun's lower lip. "Please. I want this with you. I'm okay."

Eun sucked Morgan's thumb into her mouth and then released it slowly. Morgan drew her hand back and clasped the headboard.

Eun lowered her head and kissed Morgan's clit reverently before she licked a trail down between her swollen lips. She thrust her tongue deep. Morgan arched up as Eun clung to her thighs. She thrust her tongue in and out, fucking Morgan with her tongue while she rubbed her clit hood in a slow circle with her thumb.

A harsh moan ripped from Morgan's chest. She squeezed her eyes closed as waves of pleasure roiled in her body and crashed over her, taking her breath away. She clung to the headboard, ignoring the sharp edge against her palms. She closed her eyes and savored the twin sensations of Eun's thumb on her clit and her tongue inside her. Unable to stop, Morgan came with a shout, her shoulders lifting off the bed as Eun tongue-fucked her relentlessly.

Morgan collapsed back on to the bed dizzy from her release. Eun shifted her mouth up. She flattened her tongue and pulsed it slowly against Morgan's clit. A new fire built, so sweetly intense it bordered on pain as Morgan shook thorough a second orgasm as it rippled out from her center.

"Oh, enough. Please. I can't again." Morgan licked her dry lips.

Eun lay her head on Morgan's leg. Her hair tickled where it spilled over Morgan's thigh. "You sure?" She teased one finger inside and rubbed a spot that made Morgan thrash and buck her hips for more as Eun stroked her quickly to another orgasm.

Morgan clamped her hand around Eun's wrist. "Enough." She dragged her up her body and kissed her fiercely as she rolled them over. The taste of herself on Eun's mouth flavored their kisses.

Eun dug her fingers into the muscles of Morgan's back. She sucked at her lower lip and nipped her hard. "What are you waiting for?" She rolled her hips against Morgan's body.

Morgan moved her hands down. She shoved the thin material of Eun's panties aside and thrust two fingers deep into the molten heat between Eun's legs.

Eun cupped the back of Morgan's neck as she widened her legs and rocked into her thrusts. "More. I need more." Her pupils were wide, her eyes hazy with desire.

Morgan eased another finger in as she held Eun's gaze.

"Yes. Oh yes." Eun's eyelids fluttered closed as her body opened and welcomed Morgan. Her face a mask of pleasure as liquid silk covered Morgan's fingers. She curled her fingers and pushed deeper. Eun keened and rocked up to meet Morgan's thrusts, her back arching to take all that Morgan had to give. "Harder."

Sweat pooled along Morgan's spine as she rolled her body into Eun, desperate for more sounds of her pleasure and Eun's release. The bed squeaked with their motions, and the headboard slammed the wall.

Eun wrapped her legs around Morgan's hips. "That's it. There. There."

Eun came with a long low moan, her body clutching at Morgan's fingers. Morgan lowered her head to Eun's neck and rocked slowly, easing her down. She rotated her thumb slowly over her clit.

Eun trembled under her and she clamped her hands on Morgan's shoulders. "Take it. All of it." She whispered against Morgan's skin as she came undone.

Morgan savored the sensation of Eun's surrender. The minutes stretched out. Morgan eased her fingers from Eun.

They didn't speak as Morgan shifted and lay next to Eun, sharing the pillow. The late afternoon sun painted long shadows on the wall as they lay sweaty and entangled. Eun reached down and flipped the covers over their bodies. She pressed her face into the crook of Morgan's neck and sighed.

Morgan rubbed Eun's shoulder and knew the exact moment she fell asleep. She stayed still, not wanting to wake her. Morgan's thoughts tumbled one over the other as the full weight of what they had done settled over her. *What did we do? A one-off? Something to distract her from the suck fest that is her life right now?* Morgan didn't know, and right now with Eun's warm body pressed against her and the heady scent of their afternoon tryst hanging in the air between them, she didn't want to think about it either.

Chapter Eight

Eun unlocked the door between the house and her father's office. The overhead fluorescent lights buzzed before their cool white light filled the room. Stacks of file folders spilled across the floor leading away from her father's desk. On the credenza behind his desk in a dark-walnut wood frame was her law school graduation photo.

A smaller desk was at a right angle to the wall across from her father's desk. The narrow desk was tidy. A row of small troll dolls marched along the front of the desk. A large three wick pillar candle sat on the far corner, and a heavy floral scent permeated the room.

Eun quirked her mouth at the mess. Another weirdness. Her father had been such a fanatic about appearances when she was growing up. He had burned through more than one cleaning crew with his meticulous demands. She rubbed her forehead as she stared at the messy office and tried to reconcile it with her memories of a man who had once fired a legal assistant for forgetting to empty the conference room trashcan before a client meeting.

She stepped over the piles of paperwork and sat in his worn leather chair. Eun leaned forward and placed both hands flat on the wide green blotter. *Where to start?* She turned on the computer and it hummed to life. *Please let it not be password protected.*

A tap at the outside door drew her attention. She left the desk and opened the door. "Yes?"

A short woman in a floral dress stood on the porch. "I'm sorry to bother you. You must be Eunice." She held up her keys and jingled them. "I could have let myself in, but I didn't want to startle you."

Eun studied the woman. "I'm sorry. Have we met?"

The woman fiddled with the large cross around her neck. "I'm Ginny Burns. I worked for your father."

Eun rubbed the back of her neck. "I'm sorry. I didn't know. I'm trying to sort out things. Do you get paid by check or direct deposit?"

Ginny stepped past Eun and settled the strap of her briefcase over her shoulder and entered the office. "Oh no, dear, don't worry about that right now." She gripped Eun's forearm. Her hand was soft and damp. Ginny's eyes were red-rimmed, and a glaze of tears lurked beneath their surface. Eun suppressed her shudder and stepped back, breaking contact with her.

"I wanted to see if you needed any help. It was so sudden." Ginny's eyes filled with tears, and she wiped them with the back of her hands.

"Thank you." Eun flushed. "I don't know where to start. Do you have a list of his current clients?"

"Yes. We were—he was going to sell the practice this year."

"Sell it?" Eun frowned. "He hadn't mentioned it." A fresh wave of guilt settled over her. *Was that what he wanted to talk to me about?* "I had no idea. We hadn't talked in a while."

"He always said you were busy." Ginny held on to her purse strap with both hands. The unspoken censure in her comment rankled Eun.

Ginny stepped around Eun and settled her bone-thin frame in her chair. "He stopped taking new cases six months ago. We were working to complete the ones he was working on." Her eyes watered and she sniffed loudly. "I can't believe he's gone." She wiped her eyes again.

Eun chewed her lip. "I know."

Ginny placed her purse on the floor next to her desk and glanced at Eun. "I'll do whatever I can. I'll get in touch with folks. Let them know what's happened. Get things together for when you sell it."

Eun lifted her shoulders and let them fall. "That would be good. Thank you."

"Don't worry about the practice, I'll take care of everything." Ginny rolled the wheel on a pink butane lighter and lit the candle on her desk. The cloying floral scent in the room grew stronger as it spread over the room. "I'm sure you have lots to do back in Chicago. When's the service? Your father used to belong to my husband Adam's church." She sniffed loudly.

A chill settled over Eun. She wrinkled her nose. The smell of the candle was overpowering in the small space of the office.

Eun crossed her arms over her chest. "Calling hours are Friday afternoon. Funeral on Saturday. Will you be able to get me a list of cases he was working on? And where they are in proceedings?"

Ginny drew a laptop from her bag and centered it on her desk. "I have it all right here."

Eun studied the pattern of the carpeted floor. "Thank you. I'll make sure you're paid for your time. I have a meeting with the bank this afternoon."

"I'll handle everything here." Ginny waved her hand like she was shooing flies. "Go on." She pressed a key on her laptop and gospel music filled the room. Ginny plucked a tissue from her purse and blew her nose loudly.

An itching at the base of Eun's skull made her rub her neck, and she pushed aside her unsettledness caused by Ginny's arrival. She exited back through the house and closed the door to the office space, shutting out the sound of Ginny's sniffing and the clicking of her keyboard.

*

Rudy snored, softly curled up on the rug under Morgan's desk.

"You going to leave him here? Or take him with you?" Charles sat on the tall stool behind the counter.

Morgan picked up the logbook with her day's appointments and closed it. "I'm going to leave him with you if you're okay with it. I want him to get used to staying with other people."

"You think she's gonna want him?"

"Not sure. She lives in a condo. And works a lot. So maybe not."

"You seem to know a lot about her." Her dad raised an eyebrow.

"We had lunch together." Morgan pulled her jacket from the back of the chair and ducked her head, avoiding her father's eyes. "She's kinda alone."

"No family?" Charles sipped his coffee.

"She's not on good terms with them." Morgan pressed her lips in a thin line. "She didn't say it, but I think it's a gay thing."

Her dad crossed his arms. "It amazes me how people can treat their kids that way, but Morgan"—he leaned forward on his stool—"I'm going to say this again, don't get attached to the dog. Or her."

Morgan rubbed her chin. "I know. She needs a friend right now. I can't imagine having to make all the decisions about a funeral and stuff without family."

"Her mom still around?"

"She didn't say. But her folks were divorced." She shifted her gaze to the large clock opposite the calendar. "I have to go."

Charles shifted on the tall stool behind the counter. "Fine with me. Rudy and I will hold it down."

Morgan stood up and shouldered her tool bag. "I'll be back before you close."

"Call me if you're going to be late. It's bingo night and you know how your grandma gets antsy if we don't get there fifteen minutes early. Last time I thought she was going to tuck and roll out of the truck."

Morgan laughed and settled her ball cap on her head. "I'll be back in plenty of time."

*

Eun set her luggage down on the floor of the kitchen and placed the bag of groceries on the counter. After clearing out the refrigerator she placed the eggs and loaf of bread she had purchased on the middle shelf next to a carton of oat milk. The ticking of the electric clock over the sink was loud in the quiet of the house.

She inhaled sharply and squared her shoulders before she rolled her bag through the house toward what had been her room. Eun paused outside her father's room. The bed was made, and his slippers were lined up next to the bed. His pajamas were folded in a tidy pile on top of the pillow.

Eun crossed the room and picked up his pajama top. She held it close and breathed in the scent of her father.

Tears welled up and she brushed them aside before she placed the shirt back on top of the pile. Eun left the room and didn't look back as she closed the door.

She stopped outside the door to her old room. A thousand memories flooded her mind. Shouting fights. Angry tears. The deafening click of the lock when her father would walk away and shut her in her room to study. Eun shoved the door open.

The room was empty except for a dog crate in one corner. Several dog toys were scattered around the space. Two empty dog bowls were on a plastic mat.

Eun dropped the handle of her suitcase and walked into the room. She yanked the closet door open. Her high school letter jacket, the one she had earned with speech and debate, hung on a hanger. Three plastic tubs were stacked at one end of the closet. She opened the first one. School papers and drawings with Eun's name scrawled across the top in blue crayon were on top of the pile. She replaced the lid. Each box held collections of school papers and memorabilia from Eun's school career. In the last tub, a framed copy of her law school diploma sat atop a stack of bound leather journals.

Eun sank to her knees. A hard knot rose in her throat. Visions of their argument the day she graduated rose in her memories. His stunned and furious expression after she handed him her diploma, told him she was lesbian, and walked away. Not the best way to come out but she couldn't lie anymore. Couldn't pretend to be the perfect daughter anymore.

In the fifteen years since she had come out, her father had tried every tactic he could think of to convince her she was not a lesbian. She chewed her lip as she remembered the last intervention. Her final visit home had ended when

Eun fled the house after being ambushed by members of his church he had invited to lay hands on her to cure her. She tossed the diploma back in the box and locked the lid into place.

What the hell had happened? She shouldn't be here now. He should be here. The autopsy had listed cause of death as natural. A massive coronary. *What is natural about a sixty-year-old man dying suddenly?* Eun huffed out a breath. *Probably had chest pain for years and ignored it. Always too busy to exercise. Too busy with work to be a father. Too busy for anything that was not church or work. Why'd he get Rudy? And why was he so desperate to talk to me?*

Eun pushed her hair back with her hands. She closed her hands and tugged at her hair. The sharp pull and tug on her scalp focused her. She relaxed her grip, rose on trembling legs, walked to the door, and closed it. Suitcase in tow, she pushed open the guest room door and pulled her bag inside. There was a thin layer of dust on the furniture.

She collapsed on the bed and lay back to stare at the ceiling. *What to do? Sell the house. Sell the practice. Go back to Chicago. Get back to my life. The dog. What am I going to do with the dog? Morgan'd be happy to take him. I've no time for a dog. No time. Morgan.*

Eun closed her eyes as her body heated with the memory of their afternoon together. She flattened her hands over her stomach. A dull spark flittered in her belly. They had connected. Their time together had been delicious. Sexual perfection. Eun chewed her lip. *And what the hell am I going to do about Morgan? I have no time. Will I ever have time for a partner? Hell, even time to hook up is hard to find when I'm working.* Her bank account was as full as her heart was empty.

And Morgan is more, deserves more. Eun rubbed her hands over her face. *More than I would ever be able to give. Why did I let my guard down?*

A wave of desire spread over her. She rubbed the edge of her phone. She could call Morgan. Ask her to come to the house. She could spend the evening getting lost in her golden-brown eyes and amazing body. And that would be wrong. Leading anyone on was wrong. But leading someone like Morgan on would be criminal.

Eun tossed the phone to the bed, disgusted with herself. The swirls of plaster covering the ceiling drew her eyes and her gaze followed the pattern of the random whorls. Her back ached from the soft bed at the Red Squirrel Inn almost as bad as her heart. Alone. Even after her father had cut off all communication with her, she had not been this alone. She kicked off her shoes and rolled to her side, rocking her hips to stretch her lower back. *Tired. So tired.* Eun placed her phone on do not disturb, set the alarm for an hour, and pulled the comforter over her body and pillowed her head on her arm. *Sleep. I'll adult later.*

Chapter Nine

Eun ignored how much her feet hurt in new pumps as she stood next to the long white altar covered with flowers. The simple walnut wood box containing her father's ashes was centered amid bouquets of white mums and lilies. Her Uncle Max had blown into town the night before, and Eun had successfully hidden out from him until this afternoon. Now she was the subject of her uncle's most disapproving gaze as he sat in the first row of chairs. Her father's cousins flanked him, and Eun sensed their hard stares.

"I'm so sorry for your loss." A woman Eun didn't know clasped her hand and expressed her condolences. Eun nodded and smiled at the woman. She used her best neutral courtroom face and avoided making eye contact with her.

The spicy scent of Armani Code filled her nose, and she looked up and into Morgan's eyes. Eun reached out and clasped Morgan's hand. She held tight. The sensation of her warm skin and solid touch grounded Eun. "Thank you so much for coming."

Morgan leaned closer. "I'm sorry I haven't called. I figured you'd be busy."

"A bit." Eun inclined her head toward her uncle. She leaned closer to Morgan and spoke into her ear. "Would you come to the service tomorrow? And would you mind sitting next to me?"

Morgan squeezed her hand. "I'll be there. You want me to bring the rest of the crew as buffers? My family is awesome at funeral blocks."

Eun covered her mouth with her hand to keep her smile from showing. "Any help would be appreciated. My mom's planning on coming too."

Morgan squeezed her hand once more and rubbed her thumb over the back of Eun's hand. "We'll be there."

She walked away from Eun and moved to one of the chairs in the rows at the back of the room. Eun's gaze was drawn to her wide shoulders. Dapper in a navy-blue suit over a light-blue button-down with blue-and-yellow-striped bowtie, Morgan's presence was a balm for Eun's tattered soul. *Of all the times to meet a sweet butch. Too bad.*

Eun sighed and glanced at the clock. *Thirty more minutes. I can do this. Need to slip out before Uncle Max can corner me.* Ginny Burns stopped by the altar and placed her hand on the box lid for a moment while she held her cross in her other hand. After a moment, she walked to Eun and pulled her into an embrace. "How are you holding up, dear?"

Eun extracted herself from Ginny's arms. "I'm okay. Thank you."

Ginny patted her arm. "My husband, Adam, and I will be there tomorrow. Would it be okay if he said a few words? He and your father were so close."

Eun bit her lip. "I—uh. I... Sure."

"Your father was wonderful man." Ginny smiled at her and pulled her into a second uncomfortable hug. Eun closed her eyes and breathed deep, trying to resist the urge to shove the woman off her. *Wonderful as long as you weren't queer.*

Ginny finally released her and moved along the aisle to the seats for the mourners. Eun caught Ginny's glare and followed it to Morgan. Another random person approached Eun to express their sorrow over her father's death. The afternoon wore on, and Eun tried to focus on the mourners, but her gaze continually drifted to Morgan. Her solid presence and kind expression a magnet for Eun's attention.

*

After struggling through two attempts to put on pantyhose and ripping both pairs, Eun gave up, not caring if anyone disapproved of her bare legs. She wore her hair loose and stuffed as many tissues into her purse as she could. The drive to McKnight's was short, and she parked in the spot reserved for family members. She spotted her mom's fluorescent-green VW Bug with its eyelash inserts around the headlights and rolled her eyes.

Eun rested her forehead on the steering wheel a moment and clutched the car keys in her hand. The alarm on her phone sounded. She thumbed it off with a sigh. Eun exited the car and strode to the funeral home. The air inside was cool and the scent of lilies filled the air. Eun grimaced at the smell.

"Eun?"

Cicely Park surrounded Eun in a hug. Eun stiffened in her mother's embrace, still not used to the full body hugs her mother insisted on.

"Mom." She patted her mother's back awkwardly.

Her mother stepped back and took hold of Eun's hands. "I'm sorry, dear. This must be so hard."

Eun bit her lip. "Yes."

They made their way to the room set up for the service. The minister the funeral home had recommended greeted them. His shiny bald head and oily smile made Eun's skin crawl. She stifled her urge to run from the room.

"Miss Park? So nice to meet you. I'm Reverend Atwell. I'm so sorry about your father." He grasped her hand in a limp handshake.

Eun withdrew her hand from his fleshy sweaty grip, unable to respond. Most people would assume she was overcome with sadness instead of flummoxed about what she was supposed to say.

Reverend Atwell waved toward the first row of chairs. "This is reserved for the family." Eun and her mother sat down. "I'll be back in a few minutes."

Eun leaned back into the straight-backed chair.

"I'm not sure I should sit up here." Her mother glanced at the door. "You know how Uncle Max feels about me." She smoothed a hand over her dress.

"It's fine, Mom. Sit where you're comfortable." Eun had given up counting on her mother to provide any kind of support. Her mother took a spot at the rear of the room as close to the exit as she could get. Eun stared at the walnut box containing her father's ashes. Simple and unadorned, a fitting urn for a man who eschewed ornamentation. Eun closed her eyes and folded her hands. Maybe folks would think she was praying and leave her alone. Morgan's cologne filled her senses and she opened her eyes. Morgan stood in front of her, dressed in a crisp black suit.

"Hey." Morgan tilted her head toward the row of chairs. "Where do you want us to sit?"

Eun raised her head and blinked. Officer Wright in her dark-blue full dress police uniform, flanked by a young man who looked so much like Morgan he had to be her brother, and Morgan's parents stood to the left of Morgan. "Wow. You all came. Thank you. So much, thank you." She waved to the seats around her. "Please, will you sit here?"

Morgan sat on Eun's right and Miesha sat down on her left. Her brother held his hand out and Eun clasped it. "I'm Neil, and I'm so sorry for your loss." He moved along the row of chairs and sat on the other side of Morgan.

Morgan's parents stepped in front of Eun.

"I'm Charles, and this is Margaret. We're so sorry about your father." They moved along the row and sat down next to Miesha.

Surrounded by Morgan and her family, Eun relaxed. Her eyes welled. *This, this is what it would be to have a family who loved and accepted you.* She closed her eyes and let the tears roll down her cheeks. Morgan pressed a tissue in her palm, and Eun closed her fingers around her warm hand.

A sharp suck of teeth made her open her eyes. Uncle Max towered over her. A grim expression shadowed his face.

"Eun." He glanced down the row and sniffed before he raised his chin and looked down his nose. "Who are these people?" He glared at Morgan and her family.

Eun pressed her feet to the floor and took a deep breath. "Friends." She tilted her head to the left and held her uncle's blistering glare, grateful for every hour she had ever spent deposing hostile witnesses.

Her uncle turned on his heel and made a show of plopping down two chairs away from Morgan's parents.

He straightened the seam of his bespoke suit before he crossed his legs and settled his seething glare on Eun. Morgan squeezed Eun's hand, and she shifted her gaze away from her uncle.

Ginny Burns arrived with her husband Adam in tow. He was thin and angular, his face dominated by a blade-sharp nose. A huge Bible was tucked under his arm.

"How you are holding up, darling?" Ginny's syrupy sweet voice coated Eun's ears. "I wish you'd have let us have a repast at the church. It's the least we could've done."

"It was a kind offer, but we've set things up with Ohana's to cater it here."

Ginny looked reverently at her husband. "Adam's all set as soon as the pastor asks for people to speak." She patted his arm.

Adam Burns clutched his Bible with both hands. "The lord is on me today, Miss Park. I am ready."

Eun chewed her lip and then summoned the bland smile she used on vendors whose products she wasn't buying. A few more people filed past them and filled the seats behind them.

The funeral director came in, surveyed the small gathering, and walked to Eun's place. "Do you want to wait for any more mourners, Miss Park?"

"No. It's fine. I think we should get started."

The funeral director waved at Reverend Atwell, and he made his way to the front of the room.

Eun tried to focus on his words, but she was distracted by the sense of her uncle's hard stare. The hairs on the back of her neck stayed in a constant state of arousal. She fidgeted with the tissue Morgan had handed her. Her aunt's practiced wailing at key points in the service grated on Eun's nerves. Finally, the reverend finished his part of the service. He smiled benignly at the crowd of mourners. "I have been informed Pastor Adam Burns has a few words to say."

Eun shifted her attention from the multitoned carpet to the altar. Adam Burns strode to the front of the room with his Bible clenched in his hand.

*

At first Morgan listened to Pastor Burns's words, but she lost focus as soon as he started in on "getting right with the lord" and what amounted to a sermon praising Eun's father's unflagging work against "perversion" complete with an altar call instead of a eulogy.

She studied Eun from under her lashes. Her face was pale, and her eyes were tightly closed. Eun's hands were fisted and rested on the tops of her thighs, her jaw set, the only signs of the controlled fury radiating from her body. Morgan shifted her gaze to her sister. Her arms were crossed over her chest, and she glanced at her watch twice in the few minutes Morgan observed her. Her mother and father sat holding hands. An occasional grimace crossed her mother's face.

Pride filled Morgan as she looked down the row. She had asked her family for help, and they had all agreed without any reservations. Eun was so alone. Morgan couldn't imagine how it would be to not have her family have her back. Neil nudged her foot with his shoe.

The pastor was ramping up now, his Bible clutched in one hand and the other raised to the ceiling. Ginny Burns swayed in her seat with her arms raised and a few "amens" were murmured from the others in the room. The pastor had been preaching for twenty minutes and showed no sign of slowing down.

The muscle in Eun's jaw flexed, and she was curling and uncurling her hands into fists. A soft groan reached Morgan's ears. *How to stop it? It's too much now.* Morgan turned and caught the eye of the funeral director. She subtly tapped her watch and inclined her head toward the pastor. The funeral director nodded his head in acknowledgment before he leaned close and spoke in Reverend Atwell's ear.

As Pastor Burns opened his mouth to take a breath, Reverend Atwell stepped up next to him and clapped him on the shoulder. "Thank you, brother. Let us all bow our heads for a final prayer."

Morgan covered her mouth to hide her smile at the startled expression on Pastor Burns's face. Eun's hands were knotted together in her lap. Morgan had been bold when she first arrived, using the cover of passing Eun a tissue to hold her hand. A wave of guilt washed over her. Eun was burying her father, and Morgan was thinking about how to get to hold her hand again. *What is wrong with me?* She pressed her lips into a thin line. The service wrapped up, and Eun relaxed her hands.

"The repast is being served on the lower level. Take the stairs to the left as you exit." The funeral director waved his hands at the back door of the room.

Eun stood up so fast her chair rocked, and Morgan settled it before she stood.

Eun turned to Morgan and whispered. "A few words? What the hell? That was ridiculous. All that crap about perversion. And why the hell did he have to bring up all of my dad's anti-equality work?" Her eyes flashed with rage. Tension and anger rolled off Eun in waves.

Morgan laid her hand on Eun's arm. "I'm sorry."

Eun spoke through her teeth. "The only one who should be sorry is that man. If I'd wanted to go to church, I would have."

Eun's Uncle Max approached them, bearing down on Eun, his face twisted in anger.

"Eun. What is this 'the repast is in the basement'? What kind of respect is that for your father? I knew I shouldn't have let you take care of things."

Eun spun around and faced her uncle. "But then you'd have had to pay for it, and we all know how that would go, don't we?" Her voice dripped acid.

Her uncle lifted his chin. "Always back to money. You're an ungrateful child. Your father scrimped to put you through college and law school."

"I had a full scholarship for college, uncle, and yes, he did help with law school. And I paid him back. Every single dime. Not that it's any of your business." Eun's voice dropped to a lethal tone, and her mouth pulled into a snarl. "Not sure why you think you have any right to speak to me like this." Her voice was low and deadly. Morgan tightened her fingers on Eun's arm.

Eun pulled free, flashing her a sharp glance. She stepped to her uncle, toe to toe. She loomed over him, taking advantage of her height in three-inch pumps. "You want to play it this way? Let's go."

Eun's uncle lifted his chin. "You're a terrible daughter. No wonder he was ashamed of you." An arch expression came over his face. "Wait till you find out about his will. You get nothing. Not one thing. He knew you'd use it for your disgusting lifestyle. It all goes to the church. And the house comes to me." His glare settled on Morgan before he shifted it back to Eun. "Don't think I don't know about you. You are going to hell, Eun. You and the rest of the alphabet soup of perverts." Eun's cousins had gathered around her uncle. They observed the conversation, their eyes shifting between Eun and her uncle as they shuffled their feet.

Morgan stepped between the two of them. "I don't think this is the time or place for this. And I don't care what you say about me, but you need to leave Eun alone."

Eun clasped Morgan's shoulders and moved her out of the way. "Thank you, but I don't need anyone to protect me." She shoved past her uncle, shoulder checking him, before she snatched her father's box of ashes off the table and tucked it under her arm. "Uncle, I'd say it's been nice to see you, but my father insisted on honesty." She nodded at her aunt and left without saying another word. Her strides were purposeful, and she walked out of the door leading to the foyer and the exit.

Morgan pursed her lips and crossed her arms. Miesha came and stood next to her.

Neil stepped up next to Morgan. "Problem?"

"None." Morgan turned her back on Eun's uncle and walked away from the group, trusting her siblings to block Max's path if he tried to follow Eun. She trotted in the direction Eun had taken, hoping to catch her before she left the building.

The hallway was vacant. Morgan shoved the door to the parking lot open. The slam of a car door drew her attention. The headlights on Eun's car lit up. Morgan sprinted across the parking lot. Eun pulled out of her parking space. Morgan bolted in front of the car and waved her arms. Eun swerved and stopped.

The tinted window rolled down. "What the hell is wrong with you? What do you want?" Eun shouted.

Morgan stepped closer. Eun's face was streaked with tears. "Nothing. I wanted to talk to you. To ask if you were okay, but that's a stupid question." She rested her hand on the doorframe.

Eun leaned her head against the steering wheel. "I don't have time for this. You."

Morgan lifted her hand, wanting to touch Eun's shoulder, to soothe her, before she let it fall away.

Eun raised her head and looked straight ahead, avoiding Morgan's gaze. "Thank you for coming, Morgan. And please thank your family for me. I'm sorry. I have to go." She rolled up the window. Morgan yanked her hands away to keep from getting pinched as the dark glass slid into place, blocking Eun from Morgan's view. Eun drove the car around her and sped off, gravel flying as she left the lot.

Morgan shoved her hands in her pockets. *What'd I expect? She's like a feral cat, not trusting anyone.* After witnessing the display between Eun and her uncle, and the talk of money, Morgan understood more than ever Eun's estrangement from her family. A breeze blew a yellow fast-food wrapper across the parking lot. Morgan rested her hands on her hips.

She lifted her gaze to the clear spring sky before she lowered it and studied the houses surrounding the small funeral home. Older homes most in need of paint and repair with shaggy lawns crowded the narrow brick streets. A desolate feeling settled over Morgan. *Nothing for her here. Why would she want to stay? Great sex was just that, great sex. No reason to think it might lead to more. She'll go back to her Chicago life and not give Sikesville or me a second thought.* Morgan leaned down and wiped the dust off the tips of her wingtip shoes before she walked back to the funeral home.

Chapter Ten

Eun wedged the last of the plastic tubs into the back of her car. Her young life distilled into two acrylic bins. She rested her hand on top of the bin that held her dad's journals. She'd tried looking at them the night before and failed. As much as she wanted to connect with him, it only reinforced he was gone.

Eun bit her lip. *Five years. Five fucking wasted years.* With both hands she pulled the bin out of the car and slammed it onto the driveway. *Why take it? He's gone and no amount of reading his private thoughts is ever going help me understand how he could put me out of his life.*

A loud squawk from a young crow atop the roof drew her attention to the faded remains of the flowers her dad had painted on the side door to the garage. The door led to a cozy attic play space her father had created for her. After her mother had left them, she had spent hours in the snug attic space, lying around on the old couch daydreaming, scribbling down stories, and imagining her mother would magically return.

The sun was hot on the back of her neck. She picked the box up and replaced it. Maybe if she read his words, she might understand why he never let her see her mother again, why he was so driven for Eun to succeed. Maybe one day she would be able to understand all of it. But not today.

*

Morgan ran her hands over the wood scraps laid out over Eli's bench. "Is this applewood?"

"It is." Eli moved his glasses up his nose. "I've got a bit of maple that would work for the slides."

Morgan pressed her lips together in a thin line. "I don't know what kind of wood I want to use."

Eli rubbed his fingers over the bench. "Who ya making the box for? You don't seem as into it as you were two weeks ago."

Morgan flushed. "Sorry. I don't know. Nobody."

"You have the world's worst poker face." Eli leaned back and crossed his arms. "What's up?"

Morgan traced her fingers over the graph-paper pattern. "I was going to make it for Eun."

"The one from Chicago?" Eli leaned on the workbench.

"Yes." Morgan shifted off her stool and slid the paper into a folder and tucked it under her arm. "I'll wait to make it."

Eli raised a bushy eyebrow. "She ditch ya?"

Morgan lifted a shoulder and let it fall. "Nah. Hell, I don't know. She was awkward as fuck the last time we talked. I haven't heard from her in two weeks."

Eli snorted. "Her loss." He stood and stretched. "I'm in need of a libation. Care to join me? I've got some cherry mead that's ready."

"No sir. I've got to drive home. Miesha still gives me a hard time about having to pick me up after I tried your last batch of home brew."

"Suit yourself. Come up to the house and I'll give you a bottle to take with you." Morgan followed Eli out of the shop.

*

Morgan tucked the bottle of cherry mead from Eli behind her seat. After starting the truck, she checked her phone. Her morning text to Eun had gone unanswered along with the last four texts she had sent. She turned her truck toward home. As she approached the turn for Eun's father's house she slowed the truck. A flush burned her ears as she braked hard and turned onto the street.

A woman pushing a stroller along the sidewalk glared at Morgan, and she slowed her truck to a crawl through the neighborhood. Eun's bright-red car was parked in the driveway of her father's house. Morgan rolled past, her gaze fixed on the road ahead of her, biting her lip to keep from looking back.

*

Eun woke to the sound of running water. A lot of running water. She bolted from the bed and charged into the bathroom. Nothing. And now she had to use the toilet because of the sound. Groggy, she used the toilet, and as she washed her hands, she figured it out. The basement.

The linoleum was cold on her feet as she ran through the kitchen. Eun tugged open the basement door. The sound was louder and the source evident. A water supply hose to the washer had burst and water sprayed from the remnant of the hose. *Shut-off, where is the water shut-off?* Icy-cold water wet her shirt, and she gasped. Above the washer, two pipes with twist values were mounted on the wall. Eun squinted against the spray and grabbed the rusty valve above the broken hose. Her wet hand slipped off as she attempted to turn the stubborn spigot and she cursed. She switched her grip and tried again. Nothing.

She moved away from the spray, wiping the water from her face. Eun traced the pipe's path with her gaze to the basement ceiling and followed the exposed pipes around the large room. She shivered in her drenched T-shirt and panties. On the wall opposite the washer she located a handle with a faded "water shut-off" tag wired to it.

With both hands she grabbed it and turned it. The knob resisted. She switched her grip and tried again, the sharp metal of the knob scraping her fingers and cutting her palm. Swearing loudly, she twisted it closed. The spray behind her stopped. Eun wiped her wet hair out of her face.

The basement was stacked full of cardboard banker's boxes and Eun's childhood bedroom furniture. "Just fucking great," she shouted. *One more thing to take care of. Fuck. The realtor is supposed to come today. No. I need to clean this up first.* She stormed up the steps to the guest room and snatched her phone off the table.

After dialing the realtor's number, she walked to the bathroom. Her teeth chattered, and she wrapped a towel around her shoulders. The realtor's number went to voicemail. "Hi, it's Eunice Park. I need to cancel today. Please call me back to set another appointment." She placed the phone on the vanity and then spun open the tap. A trickle of water ran out and then nothing. *Right. Water's off.* Eun pinched the bridge of her nose. *Great. Just fucking great. I need to go back to Chicago.* She grimaced when she thought back to her phone call with Heather and how she had reluctantly agreed to Eun taking another week to settle her father's affairs.

Her bag was packed. She would leave immediately after the meeting with the executor of her father's will. It had not been as her uncle had screamed at the funeral. Eun was the sole heir to everything. She could close the door on this house, leave the keys with a realtor, walk away from Sikesville, and never have to think about it again. Except she would. She would replay her idiocy with Morgan in the parking lot after the funeral in her memories for the rest of her life. The sad shocked expression on Morgan's face was etched on her retinas. She had shoved Morgan away, not wanting to have any reason to ever be in Sikesville again.

She clenched her jaw to stop her teeth from chattering as she tugged her wet shirt over her head and pulled off her underwear. She balled the clothes up and walked back to the guest room. After sorting through her suitcase, she dressed in T-shirt, jeans, and a flannel overshirt. Still shivering, she flopped onto the bed and wrapped the quilt around her body.

Morgan. She could call Morgan. She would come. And help. And gaze at Eun with those patient warm eyes, and Eun would be even more confused about what to do. She flushed, remembering the awkwardness of their conversation when she had called to apologize for leaving her in the funeral parking lot. A phone call punctuated by heavy silences as they ignored the unspoken what-ifs between them.

Eun rolled to her back and rested her hands on her stomach. She had begged off the two times Morgan had called and asked her to have coffee, not trusting herself to keep it at that, not wanting to let herself indulge in the gloriousness of Morgan's body.

Morgan was rooted to this town and her family. Eun was alone. An orphan. Her mother, for all her words of support, had hightailed it back to Columbus and her clients as soon as the funeral was over. She had not called Eun since the funeral. The irony of her mother's ability to comfort complete strangers and not her daughter washed over Eun. She twisted her hands in the blanket. Her mother would never change, and Eun had wasted too many years imagining she would.

"Get it together, Park." Eun spoke out loud, her words hollow in her ears. Eun was a lot of things, but a user was not one of them. She was leaving, and it wasn't right to lead Morgan or herself on. Eun left the guest room and went to the kitchen. The walnut box with her father's ashes rested in the middle of the kitchen table. "What to do, Dad?"

Would it be so bad to call her? Eun shivered when she thought about how she had enjoyed their lunch date, how titillating her flirtatious banter. Morgan was solid and clever and kind. Eun would never be able to express to her how much she appreciated her presence at the funeral. Without her quiet strength and the support of Morgan's family, she would not have been able to sit through the funeral.

Eun drummed her fingers on the table. Ginny, in spite of her husband's ridiculous behavior at Eun's father's funeral, had been indispensable. But her presence disturbed Eun so much she set aside the idea of calling her for help. She fiddled with the stack of bank statements on the table. After looking at her father's accounts, Eun wondered how he had stayed in business. Of particular concern were large monthly cash withdrawals he made without matching receipts. He'd always been meticulous about his accounts. Eun had spent more than one Saturday night with her father at the kitchen table as they worked on reconciling both the family and business ledgers.

Her father's account books, kept in his careful print, were in the dining room hutch where he had always kept them. Noticeable in its absence was the business account book. Eun wondered who had finally convinced her father to use accounting software. Eun had spent most of last night sending out billing notices along with notices of her father's passing and suggestions for other attorneys to take over the cases he had been working on.

In the midst of sorting her father's practice, she had been in constant contact with Sally working on her own cases. She ground her teeth as she thought about trusting her idiot associate to keep up with important dates. She pinched the bridge of her nose. A headache. She had missed dinner last night and breakfast this morning. No coffee. And now she had a flooded basement to clean up.

Eun glanced at her phone. Sunday. What would it cost to get a plumber on Sunday? She could wait, but then she'd have to go without water until tomorrow. Morgan. Morgan would know. And would come and help her if she asked. And who else could she call? And the idea of meeting the executor over the conference table without a shower made her shudder. She picked up her phone and texted Morgan.

*

Morgan's phone buzzed and she laid her book facedown on the coffee table before she swiped her phone off the end table. Rudy shifted on her belly, resettled his muzzle under her chin. She shifted on the couch trying not to disturb him as she read the text.

> *I need help. I feel bad asking, but I have a flood in the basement.*

Morgan chewed her lip. She had invited her to coffee twice, and Eun had not responded. Morgan had checked her phone at least twenty times a day, thinking she might have missed a call, but no. Radio silence, and by the end of two weeks she wondered if Eun was still in town. Curious, she had driven past her father's house. Disappointment had warred with annoyance after she spotted Eun's car in the driveway.

She scratched Rudy behind his ears. She knew Eun wouldn't be taking him, so she had placed her application to adopt him as soon as Eun let the shelter know he was available. Every moment she spent with Eun reminded Morgan she was nothing to Eun other than a pleasant afternoon diversion.

Morgan had been willing, more than willing to be a distraction even if her stupid heart was still bruised. Rudy snuggled closer, and Morgan sighed. As a consolation prize she had to admit Rudy was awesome, but a girlfriend would be better.

The phone buzzed again, a call this time. Morgan picked up the call.

"Morgan?"

"Yeah." Morgan rested her hand on Rudy's back and ruffled his fur.

"I'm sorry I haven't called before this."

"S'all right." It wasn't, but what to say? Morgan waited.

"Can you give me the name of a good plumber?"

"What happened? Why do you need one?" Morgan moved Rudy off her and sat up.

"The washer water supply hose burst."

"Did you get the water shut off?" Morgan stood up. Hearing the desperation and anxiety in Eun's voice made her chest hurt.

"Yes. It took me a while to find it, but I got it shut off."

"Thalia Makris is good, but unless you want to replace the water shut-offs, you don't need her. You need to replace the washer hoses. It's an easy fix."

"What's the best place to get new supply hoses on a Sunday?"

"The big box store on Thirty is open." Morgan scrubbed her hand over her face. "You want me to come over and take a look?"

"I don't want to disturb your Sunday any more than I have."

The hesitation in Eun's voice grated against Morgan's ear, and she drummed her fingers on her knee. "I'm not busy. And I didn't have any plans."

"It would be fantastic, but please don't do it out of obligation. I'm a grown woman. I know how to use tools and YouTube to fix things."

"But do you know where your dad's tools are? I could bring mine over. Save you buying a wrench."

"I would be the most grateful woman on the face of the earth if you could come over and help. I haven't looked for tools. My dad always called other folks to fix things."

"I'll be there in fifteen." *Easy. I'm so damn easy.*

"Morgan?"

"Yeah?"

"Thank you. Really, thank you."

"See ya soon." Morgan disconnected the call. "Come on, Rudy. You need to come with me, so I don't do anything stupid."

Rudy sat up and snorted before he slid belly first off the couch.

More stupid. Her heart chastised her. Sure, Eun had called her when she needed something. Not because she missed Morgan. She hadn't even called to see if she could spend time with Rudy. Morgan knew she was going to walk away from both of them.

Rudy yawned and blinked at her.

Morgan stroked his fur. "Let's go, boy." She strode out of her living room and snagged her jacket off its peg in the kitchen. Rudy sat while she snapped his leash on, and they trotted down the stairs together.

Chapter Eleven

Rudy's barking signaled Morgan's arrival. Eun shrugged aside her anxiety over seeing her again. She trotted up the basement steps and to the back door. She opened the door and held it wide. Rudy scooted past Eun and ran to where his dog bowls had been. He shot Eun a dirty look over his shoulder and sniffed around the spot before he lay down on the rug in front of the sink. Morgan stepped inside. In spite of her desperation to feel her solid energy and steadiness, Eun gripped the seam of her jeans and resisted pulling Morgan into a hug.

Morgan waved. "Hey." She inclined her head toward the basement steps. "I'll go take a look." She quirked her mouth at Rudy. "And he has had his breakfast no matter what he tells you. I've got him on diet food, and he hates it."

Eun rested her hands on her hips. "Speaking of food, can I take you to brunch?"

Morgan pursed her lips. "Were you feeling awkward about us and lied about the washer hose to get me over here?"

"What? No. I need to eat before I deal with anything. I can't even fucking make coffee." Eun looked away from Morgan. "I'm not that kind of person, Morgan. If I'd wanted to see you, I wouldn't have made something up."

Morgan pressed her lips together in a thin line and looked away from Eun.

"I mean—that's not what I—" Eun grabbed her hair with both hands and shoved it away from her face. "I didn't mean—"

"I get it. Sorry, I said anything." Morgan walked down the basement steps.

An annoyed yip startled Eun, and she glared at Rudy. "I know I fucked up. You don't have to tell me."

Eun hugged her arms around herself. *Why? Why I am I like this?*

She bolted down the basement steps. Most of the water had drained out of the rear floor drain. Scattered puddles of water spread out over the concrete. Eun walked gingerly between them to keep her shoes dry.

Morgan was crouched down behind the washer detaching the remnant of the hose, her face a stony mask.

Eun leaned over the washer and tapped Morgan on the shoulder. "Stop."

Morgan stood up with the wrench in her hand. "You want to do it?"

"No." Eun took the wrench from Morgan's hand and placed it on top of the washer. "No. I don't."

Morgan frowned. "What then?"

"This." Eun stepped around the washer. She reached up and cupped Morgan's face with both hands and kissed her.

Morgan held herself stiff in Eun's arms. Her mouth was rigid at first, and Eun kissed her gently and rubbed her cheekbone with her thumb. Morgan grabbed Eun's hips and pulled her tight to her as a flare of heat blazed between them.

Her kiss was hard, bruising, and everything Eun craved. Eun broke their kiss and peered into Morgan's eyes. "I'm so sorry. So very sorry. I wasn't trying to hurt you." She leaned her forehead against Morgan's chest. "I wanted to call you so many times."

"Why, Eun?" Morgan pushed Eun back so she could peer into her face. "Why did you ghost? Afraid I'd want more? That I'd try and keep you here? For fuck's sake, I'm a grown-ass woman. I'm not some clingy kid. I know you have a life. And I know you're going to go back to Chicago. I didn't ask you for anything."

"I didn't want you to think I was using you."

Morgan pulled away from Eun. "So, driving away from me and then ghosting was your way to make me think you weren't? What kinda fucked-up logic is that? At least give me some agency in this. I may not have gone to college, but I'm not stupid, Eun. I know"—she gestured between them—"whatever this is, it's not forever."

Eun pushed her hair back with both hands. "I didn't know what to do after my dad's funeral. And I'm not myself right now, so could you cut me a break? I'm not the best at relationships."

"Understatement."

"It's not like I've had a bunch of girlfriends. I don't know how to do this."

Morgan stepped back and rested her hands on her hips. "Girlfriend? What the hell? We slept together once and had some fun chats."

Eun's face burned. "And now you've made it clear you wouldn't be interested in me like that, why were you so mad I didn't call you?"

Morgan looked away. "I don't even know. It's not like it would ever work out, so that's on me."

Eun stepped into Morgan's space and took her hands and laced their fingers together. She tugged hard and pulled Morgan close. "Why? Why not?"

Morgan leaned her forehead on Eun's brow. "Because that's not what you want."

Eun lifted her chin and kissed Morgan gently on the lips. "You don't know what I want. Hell, I don't know what I want. But this with you feels amazing. And it scares the hell out of me. I'm forty-two years old, and I've only had two serious relationships. Both were unmitigated disasters. I haven't been in a relationship since I was twenty-eight."

Morgan hugged her close. "That's a long time."

Eun relaxed into Morgan's embrace. "It is. And it became comfortable. I don't have any idea what a functional relationship looks like. My parents fought all the time. I fell asleep to them yelling at each other more often than not. One time my mom chased my father out of the house with a knife. They split when I was six. I went to school one day, came home, and my mom was gone. Everything. Her clothes, photos of us. Every single thing. My father never told me why and acted like I was being ridiculous if I cried about it."

Morgan rubbed her back in slow circles. "I can see how that would scare you off of relationships, but Eun, you are not them. And no matter where this goes between us, you're safe with me. Always."

Eun leaned into Morgan's warmth. "I can't promise you anything."

"Not asking you to. I'm asking you give us a chance." Morgan held Eun at arm's length. "And keep talking to me. Don't shut me out again. Please. No matter where this goes, I'm your friend, Eun."

Eun held Morgan's gaze. "I can do that."

Morgan released her and picked up the wrench. "I'll get these hoses disconnected and see what length we need to buy. Go get ready."

"For what?"

"For breakfast and a run to the hardware store."

*

The Appletree diner was packed with the after-church crowd. Morgan led the way to the hostess desk.

"Hey there, stranger. I can seat you at the counter if you want to eat right now." Joann, the hostess, called to Morgan.

Morgan nodded her head toward where Eun was waiting. "Got two seats?"

Joann turned and surveyed the counter. "In five. Bill and Doris are paying now."

Morgan walked back to Eun. "It'll be few minutes. You're okay with the counter, right?"

Eun set aside the newspaper she had been reading. "I'd sit on the curb if they would serve me coffee. I have a ripping headache."

Morgan nodded. "Caffeine headaches are the worst."

"Morgan," Joann called and waved at them. They crossed the room, dodging children as families milled about waiting for a table or a coveted booth.

Morgan sat and Eun perched on the stool next to her, elbow to elbow at the narrow counter. She plucked a plastic menu card from between the napkin holder and the sugar shaker and passed it to Eun.

"Morning, ladies."

"Morning, Shirley. This is Eun. Eun, Shirley."

Shirley nodded at Eun. "Morning, and nice to meet you." She placed two cups in front of them along with two rolls of silverware. "Coffee?"

"Nice to meet you, and yes, please." Eun answered before Morgan could say anything.

Shirley turned back from them and returned with a carafe of coffee. She filled their cups. "You want your regular?"

Eun turned to Morgan. "Do you know everyone in town?"

Morgan laughed. "No. Not everyone. But I do know a lot of folks. Shirley's the owner, and we've done some work for her."

"What'll you have, honey?"

"What is your usual?" Eun turned to Morgan and pursed her lips.

"Two eggs over medium, two bacon, two pancakes, with a side of fried mush."

Eun raised an eyebrow. "Too much food for me." She turned to Shirley. "Two eggs over easy with two bacon, please, and toast."

"White, whole wheat, or rye?"

"Rye, and a glass of water. Please." Eun lifted her coffee cup to her mouth and took a large swallow.

"Got it." She reached under the counter. She placed a bottle of hot sauce and a squeeze bottle of ketchup next to it on the counter before she left them. Morgan leaned her leg against Eun's thigh under the counter.

Eun turned to her, holding her gaze over the rim of her coffee cup. "Yes?"

"Just wanted to look at you." Morgan folded her hands together on the countertop.

Eun rolled her eyes. "Are you always this sappy?"

"Yep. And you like it."

Eun laughed. "Yeah, I do. I feel like I've been out of touch with so much. All I've ever done is work my ass off. First at school and then at the firm."

"Tell me about your job. What kind of law do you do?"

The server walked past with the coffee carafe and refilled Eun's cup. Eun took a sip and set it aside. "I'm a litigator."

"And what does that mean?"

"I'm a trial lawyer for civil cases."

"Do you like it?" Morgan raised her eyebrow.

"Well enough." Eun's stomach clenched when she thought of her recent loss.

"You sure? You don't sound like you're sure."

Eun placed both hands flat on the counter. "Now that I've done it, I don't know if I would do it again if I were at the beginning of my career."

Their breakfasts arrived. Morgan dotted her eggs with hot sauce.

"Pass me that when you're done, please."

Eun took the hot sauce from Morgan and adorned her own eggs. They ate in silence for a few minutes, the bustle of the restaurant around them increased.

Morgan looked up and over Eun's head toward the lobby of the restaurant. "Good thing we got here when we did. The line is out the door now."

Eun swiped her plate with the last of her toast and then popped it into her mouth. "My head is starting to feel better. Thank you." She gulped her water.

Morgan cut a corner off her fried mush cake. "You sure cleaned your plate fast. You want some of this?"

Eun tilted her head to the side. "Isn't this how everything started with us?"

Morgan pushed the plate of mush between them. A large hand clamped on her shoulder.

"What er you doin'?" Her brother's deep bass voice in her ear made her start. Morgan bumped her coffee cup, and it spilled across the counter.

"Damn it, you asshole."

Neil laughed and grabbed some napkins from the dispenser and wiped up the counter. "Sorry, sis. Hi, Eun."

"Hi. You're Neil, right?" Eun held out her hand.

Neil nodded to her. "I'd shake your hand, but right now I've got soggy napkins in them."

"Neil Wright, are you causing problems again?" Shirley mock glared at Neil.

"You know it."

"Give me those." Shirley took the soggy napkins from Neil's hand. "You want something?"

"You know what I want."

"Well, you'll have to get in line, but do you want any food?"

Morgan guffawed.

Neil clasped both hands over his heart. "You wound me, Shirley. I'll settle for a scrambled eggs and sausage plate if I can't have you."

"Sit. You want coffee?"

Neil yawned. "No. I'm on my way home to sleep. Orange juice, please."

Eun dabbed her mouth with her napkin. Morgan frowned at her brother. "Other than scaring the hell out of me, what's on your agenda beside sleeping? You going to be at Mom's for dinner tonight?"

"Yeah. You guys going to be there?"

Morgan huffed. "I don't know."

Eun rested her hand on Morgan's arm. "It's okay if you had plans."

Morgan covered Eun's hand with her own. "Would you want to brave Sunday dinner with my folks?" Morgan tensed her shoulders ready for Eun to decline as she saw the panic and fear sweep over her face.

"Sure." Eun gripped Morgan's arm. "I can do that."

Morgan sensed Neil watching her for a response. She turned to him. "We'll be there."

"Cool. I'll let Mom know to set another plate." Shirley slid Neil's breakfast plate in front of him. He picked up the hot sauce and covered his eggs with it.

Shirley reached into her pocket. "Separate or together."

"Sep—"

"Together." Eun spoke over Morgan. "Let me. You're going to show me how to fix the washer."

"Okay. If you're sure."

"I'm sure."

Morgan shrugged into her jacket. She bumped Neil with her shoulder. "See ya."

Eun picked up the breakfast bill. "Nice seeing you again, Neil."

"See you at dinner." Neil waved his fork at them.

Chapter Twelve

"Don't overtighten it or you'll flatten the washer, and it'll leak." Morgan handed Eun the hose to attach to the washer.

"Got it." Eun lined up the bright steel-covered cable and attached it as Morgan looked on.

She stood up from behind the washer. With Morgan guiding her she finished attaching the hoses to the water supply.

"All right. You stay there. I'll turn the water on. If it starts leaking holler and I'll turn it off."

Eun dried her hand on her pants legs. "Okay."

The hoses twitched when the water flowed into them. Eun chewed her lip while she waited to see if they would leak.

"All good?"

"All good. Should I check it by turning the washer on too?"

"Wouldn't hurt." Morgan came and stood next to Eun. She tapped the two pipes leading into the washer. "You should get new shut-offs on these. That way if there's a problem you don't have to shut down the water to the whole house."

Eun stood up and passed the wrench to Morgan. "Thank you. I will."

Morgan gestured to the wet boxes and debris scattered over the basement floor. "You want me to help you with this?"

Eun glanced around at the mess. "No. I'm done for the day. And don't we have to get ready to go to your mom's house?"

Morgan rubbed the back of her neck.

The doubt and fear in her eyes undid Eun. "If you still want me to come, that is. I know Neil put you on the spot."

"I'd love for you to come to dinner." Morgan looked away from Eun's eyes. "I don't want you to feel like you owe me."

Eun sucked in a breath. "I'm not doing it out of obligation. I want to. Your family made my father's funeral so much easier."

Morgan scuffed her boot on the floor. "They did it as a favor to me. If you're sure. You want me to come back and pick you up?"

Eun crossed to where Morgan stood. "Hey, look at me."

Morgan raised her eyes to Eun, her face expressionless.

"I'm not a player, Morgan. I don't have game other than in a courtroom. I meant what I said before."

"There's one more thing. Neil's fiancée, Cecelia, is trans."

"And? Why are you telling me this?" Eun held Morgan's gaze.

Morgan shrugged. "Some people would be bothered." A frown passed over her face. "Or be rude about it."

"I'm not some people. And I'm happy for your brother and Cecelia." She reached out and clasped Morgan's hand. "Come upstairs. I won't be long if you don't mind waiting."

Morgan pulled Eun close. "Nope. I'll wait."

Eun wrapped her hands in Morgan's shirt and kissed her. Morgan's hand cupped the back of her neck and she sighed into Eun's mouth. The sound sent a wave of want through her and told Eun more than words how long Morgan was willing to wait for her.

Eun slid her hands around and grabbed two handfuls of Morgan's wonderful ass. She kissed her along her jaw and under her ear. "What if I get my clothes and we shower at your place?"

Morgan wrapped her arms tighter around Eun. "That sounds like a plan. I'll walk Rudy. Get your things. Your pajamas too. If you plan on wearing any."

Eun nipped Morgan's ear. "I won't be. Not if I'm lucky."

"I'd say there's a ninety percent chance of that."

Eun flicked her tongue over Morgan's skin. "Only ninety percent?" She nipped Morgan. "What the hell?"

Morgan laughed. "Well, you know if we stay up late, or something. We might be too tired."

Eun rocked her hips into Morgan. "Maybe we should take care of things beforehand."

Morgan smiled against her mouth. "Maybe."

Rudy's frenzied alarm bark startled them both and they broke apart. Morgan took the stairs two at a time. "I haven't heard him like that since the first time I met him."

Eun followed on Morgan's heels. Rudy was standing in front of the back door with his hackles raised, barking viciously.

"Rudy, hush!" Morgan crossed to the door and looked out of the peephole. A loud knocking sounded again.

"I know you're home, Eun. Open this door."

Morgan reached for the doorknob.

"No."

Morgan backed away from the door, caught Rudy by his collar, and held on to him.

"We have nothing to discuss, Uncle Max. See you at the meeting tomorrow. Leave, or I'll call the police." Eun shouted through the door.

"I want to talk to you now. You owe me. I'm family."

Rage at his demand swept through Eun. She snatched the interior door open, leaving the screen door in place. "How dare you? I owe you? Family? No, Max. 'Family' does not take advantage of family. 'Family' does not abandon children. And most of all 'family' is not you. Fuck you. And fuck you for saying you're 'family.' Get off my porch. Now." She held up her phone. "You have exactly one minute to get away from here, or the police will explain trespassing to you."

Eun's uncle sputtered.

"Down to forty-five seconds." Eun waved the phone in the air, her finger hovering over the keypad.

Max huffed, spun on his heel, and stomped away from the house.

Eun trembled and rubbed at the pain in her stomach.

Rudy whined and Eun turned at the sound. Morgan was kneeling next to him stroking him softly.

"He really hates your uncle."

Eun frowned. "Yeah. Which is weird. My uncle and my dad used to spend every Sunday together. When I was home, we all had to go to church together, and then we'd all have Sunday dinner together. My cousins hated it. I hated it."

Morgan rose to her feet. "I'll walk Rudy. Get your stuff. I don't want you to have to deal with him again."

"I'll only be a moment. I'm packed already."

Morgan pressed her lips together in a thin line. "You're leaving tomorrow?"

Eun swallowed hard. "That was my plan."

"Was?"

"Was." Eun cupped Morgan's face and kissed her softly.

*

Morgan opened the door to the apartment. Rudy waddled ahead of them, promptly sat, and waited for his leash to be removed. Eun unsnapped his leash. "Where should I put this?"

Morgan waved toward the coat rack. "Clip it on the hat rack."

Eun clipped the leash to the wrought iron stand. "Done. Now you said something about a shower?"

Morgan grinned and walked backward toward the hall. "This way."

Eun followed Morgan down the short hallway to the bathroom.

"Towels and washcloths are in the cabinet."

Eun pulled her toiletries bag from the front pocket of her roller bag. "Thank you. What's the dress code for tonight?"

"Clothes."

Eun raised an eyebrow and tilted her head to the side. "I assumed your folks weren't nudists."

"Wear what you're comfortable in. I'm wearing jeans if that helps you decide."

Eun grimaced. "I don't have any clean jeans. Will a skirt be too much?"

Morgan leaned close and kissed the corner of Eun's mouth. She curled her arm around her waist, tugged her close, and kissed her again before she answered. "Not for me." She cupped Eun's ass and squeezed.

Eun turned her head, giving Morgan access to her neck. And Morgan breathed in the subtle scent of sweat and Eun's skin, new and yet familiar. She nuzzled her way along her neck. "Shower. If you don't get in now, I'm going to make us late."

Eun dropped her toiletries bag to the floor and wrapped her arms around Morgan's neck. "Oh no. You don't get to kiss me like that and walk away." She dug her fingers into the back of Morgan's neck and kissed her fiercely.

Morgan's clit stiffened, and her briefs flooded with pent-up desire from their afternoon together. Eun tugged her shirt from her pants and drew her short nails across Morgan's lower back. Gooseflesh rose along her arms. Eun kissed her as she moved her hands to the front of Morgan's jeans, yanked her belt open, slipped the button free, and slid the zipper down. Morgan shifted her hips to give her room. Eun pressed her against the wall. She broke their kiss and leaned back to see into Morgan's face, her eyes dark with desire. She swept her fingers over her wet curls and brushed against her clit. Morgan panted.

Eun rubbed in quick circles and Morgan gripped her shoulders as the pleasure spiraled out from her center. Eun sucked on her earlobe. She dipped lower and teased a finger into Morgan. Morgan tried to widen her stance, limited by the fabric of her jeans. Eun moved back to her clit, the slick roughness of her finger a sweet torture. Morgan groaned as Eun drew out her pleasure.

Eun kissed the hollow of Morgan's throat before she nipped her. Morgan's hips rocked with Eun's attentions.

"Give it to me, baby. I want you to come for me." Eun's whisper feathered across the skin of her neck.

Morgan closed her eyes and let herself be swept along by Eun's sweet touch as she worked her clit. She came with a sharp cry and groan.

Eun pulled her hand free and cupped Morgan. She squeezed hard. An aftershock ricocheted through Morgan's body. Eun kissed her gently before she let her go. She picked up her toiletries bag. She turned and patted Morgan's cheek before she walked into the bathroom and closed the door. "Out in a minute."

Morgan rested her head against the wall and closed her eyes. Unaccustomed to being taken, she basked in the feeling of being the object of Eun's desire and attention and wondered how she could convince Eun to stay for longer than a night.

*

The spicy smell of cumin and chilies wafted out when Morgan opened the door to her parents' house. Eun stepped in after her. "Let me have your coat." She helped Eun off with her coat and hung both their coats in the hall closet. She led her along the narrow hallway to the large kitchen opening on to the dining room. The table was set with seven place settings.

"Hey, you made it!" Neil called from his chair at the dining room. "Good to see you, Eun."

Margaret turned from the stove. "Welcome, Eun."

Eun held out the bouquet of flowers she had made Morgan stop so she could buy. "These are for you. And thank you. I don't know the last time I had home-cooked food."

Morgan's mom took the bouquet. "These are lovely. Morgan, grab a vase out of the china hutch."

Morgan left to get the vase.

"Is there anything I can help with, Missus Wright?"

"No. And it's Margaret. Everything is ready. We're waiting for Neil's Cecelia then we can eat."

"Where's Pop?" Morgan placed the heavy green glass vase on the counter.

"Out in the garage. He saw some organizing show and he's out there determined to get rid of whatever doesn't 'spark joy.'"

Morgan raised her eyebrow. "For real?"

Margaret stirred a large pot with a long wooden spoon. "Yes. And I'm worried. He promised to not get rid of any of my Christmas decorations, and to ask if it's something we both use."

Eun fidgeted next to Morgan, the back of her hand brushing against her fingers. Morgan took her hand and squeezed her fingers once. "I'm going to have a beer. What do you want to drink, Eun?"

"Water is fine."

Morgan left Eun standing by the counter and crossed to the refrigerator and found a beer for herself. "You want ice?"

"No. Thank you."

Morgan brought the water pitcher to the counter and plucked a glass from the cabinet. She filled a glass.

"Go sit with Neil. I'm good here." Margaret shooed them out of the kitchen.

Neil tapped the table next to his seat. "Eun, come sit by me. I didn't get to talk to you at all at breakfast."

Eun slid around the edge of the table and sat down next to Neil. Morgan sat next to Eun and leaned around her and slapped the back of his hand. "Behave yourself, or I will tell Cecelia all about the time you brought a bucket of caterpillars in the house to watch *He-Man*."

Eun giggled. "A bucket?"

"It was a little red sand pail. I was four."

Morgan laughed. "I wish I had a video of Mom when she realized the caterpillars were not into He-Man and had crawled out of the bucket and were all over our den."

Neil shook his head. "All right. And I'm pretty sure you already told her that one. What if I tell Eun about you sending me down the stairs using Mom's ironing board as a sled."

Eun raised both brows. "No." Eun turned to Morgan. "You did that?"

"Yes." Neil pointed to a small scar over his brow. "Oh yes, she did."

"Truce." Morgan tapped the table. "We don't need to bore Eun with our stories."

"All right." Neil leaned back in his chair. "Okay. So, Eun, what do you do for fun?"

"Fun?" Eun raised an eyebrow.

"Yeah. Like a hobby. What do you do when you're not working?"

Eun lifted a shoulder and let it fall. "Read. Mostly."

Neil rubbed his hands together. "What do you read? I warn you we are a family of strong literary opinions."

Eun laughed. "I like a good police procedural, thrillers mostly."

"You and Mom. I'm a sci-fi and high fantasy reader. Morgan is eclectic, you never know what she's going to be reading. Last week it was something about the natural history of earthworms."

"Hey, it was good. And the title alone was worth reading it."

Eun shifted in her seat to peer into Morgan's face. "What was the title?"

"*The Earth Moved: On the Remarkable Achievements of Earthworms.*"

Eun raised her eyebrow. "Sounds riveting."

Neil guffawed. "Right? Give me some sandworms eating folks any day."

Morgan rolled her eyes at her brother's teasing. "It was interesting."

"You still have the compost worm bin under your sink?" Neil touched Eun's arm. "She's a frustrated farmer."

"Nah, I didn't have enough scraps to feed them. I put them in the compost bin here."

The sound of the front door opening made them all glance up. A woman dressed in maroon scrubs and carrying a large shoulder bag entered. She hugged Morgan's mom before she turned to them. She strolled over, leaned down, and brushed a quick kiss over Neil's lips.

She held out her hand. "You must be Eun. Neil said you might be here. I'm Cecelia."

Eun clasped Cecelia's hand. "So nice to meet you."

Cecelia nodded at Morgan. "Hey, you. Marilyn asked about you."

A fierce flush crept up Morgan's neck and her ears burned. "She did?" Her voice squeaked and she took a sip of her beer.

"She wanted to climb in the car with me when I said you'd be here." Cecelia waved her long fingers in the air and arched her eyebrow. "Said to tell you to call her."

Morgan sensed Eun's gaze on her and her withdrawal as if it were physical.

"I'll call her." Morgan reached under the table and rolled her napkin between her fingers.

A chill descended over the room. Morgan looked away from Eun's tight smile and stiff posture.

Neil stood up abruptly and caught Cecelia's hands. "Come on, baby. I want to—show you the garage. Dad's been organizing it. You'll love it."

Cecelia held up her bag. "Wait. I want to change first."

Neil laid his hand on her arm. "Great. Yes. Come on." And he dragged her from the dining room.

Morgan scrubbed her hand over her face. "It's not like Cecelia made it sound."

Eun traced her finger around the base of her glass. "It's fine. I don't expect anything, Morgan."

Morgan reached over and stilled her hand. "I'm telling you it was not a thing with Marilyn. We went out once. Two weeks after I met you. I thought you had gone back to Chicago. If I had wanted to see more of her, I would have called her."

"She obviously has fond memories of your date." The ice in Eun's voice was sharp.

Morgan sighed and looked up at the ceiling. "I had chat sex with her after our date, yes, but that was it. I didn't want more. And I should have let her know."

Eun stared straight ahead, her silence as loud as a shout. Morgan clasped her hands together. "I'm sorry I didn't tell you. I didn't think it was important."

Eun turned to her. "It's not. I'm fine. You had a life before I arrived, Morgan. You'll have one after I go. It's fine."

Morgan bit her lip. "It's not the same. With you."

"What's not the same? I'm fine with casual sex, Morgan."

Morgan sipped her beer. "What if I'm not?"

Eun straightened her posture. "I can't promise you anything more right now. I'm going back to Chicago. You and I both are old enough to know long-distance relationships are not—" Her words faded out. She turned, cupped Morgan's face, and brushed a kiss over her lips. "Let it go. I'm fine. Let's have dinner and pretend we're a happy couple, okay?"

Morgan's gut roiled over the sadness in Eun's eyes and the resignation in her voice.

"Who's ready to eat?" Her mother's shout from the kitchen broke the moment. Eun moved her hands back to her lap. Morgan's face burned from where Eun's fingers had rested on her cheeks. Her heart in tatters, Morgan stood up. "I'll go get the rest of them."

*

The dinner had been interminable. Eun worked hard to keep up her façade of happiness amid the too-perfect family meal. The food was delicious, the siblings didn't fight, and they all told delightful stories about each other. Eun laughed politely, and yet, the entire meal she wanted to flip the table.

As much as Eun wanted to believe Morgan about wanting more with her, the stark evidence of Morgan having sex, even if it was cybersex, with someone even as she and Eun were in the midst of whatever it was they were doing was difficult to ignore. *How can I blame her? I ghosted. What did I expect would happen? That she would be fine with that? And stay celibate forever? Wait for me to get my head out of my ass?*

A touch on her arm brought her out of her thoughts. "Sorry, what?"

"Are you ready to go? I know you have a big day tomorrow." Morgan's eyes were dark.

"If you're ready. I know you enjoy your family."

"I can see them anytime. I want to take advantage of what time I have left with you."

Eun pressed her lips together in a thin line. "Of course." *Like we are going back to have wild sex? So she can rock my world. And leave me hungry for what I'm never going to have?*

Eun forced a smile as she said goodbye to Morgan's family, more than ready to leave the awkwardness of their dinner behind. She tucked her hands under her thighs on the ride home. Moonlight bathed the car with white light, and Eun studied Morgan's profile as she drove them back to her apartment. Eun shifted in her seat anxious to be in Morgan's arms, determined to let go of her hurt, desperate for Morgan to brand Eun with her touch, for her to gift Eun with glorious moments to remember after she returned to her drab solo life.

Chapter Thirteen

Rudy voiced his displeasure when they entered Morgan's apartment.

Morgan grabbed his leash off the hat rack and clipped it on him. "I need to walk him before bed. Back in a few."

Eun nodded her agreement. After the door closed, she took off her coat and placed it on the coat rack. She hung her purse over the arm of the chair and rolled her suitcase into the living area. The room was lined in bookshelves. Stacks of books overflowed onto the floor around them. In one corner of the room a collection of wooden boxes crowded the shelves. A small flat-screen television stood on a low stand with video discs scattered about it.

The small couch was barely bigger than a love seat and a crocheted afghan hung over the back of it. Eun perched on the edge of the love seat. *What do I do? I want to have her strong body under me, to feel her surrender, cherish her.* Her heart twinged as she thought about their uncomfortable dinner. She pushed aside thoughts of Morgan with someone else as she unbuttoned her shirt and untucked it. *Shower.* A shower to wash away her worries and all the what-ifs plaguing her. *It is what it is, nothing more. Great sex doesn't mean we're compatible any other way. Even if she likes to read as much as I do and laugh at the same things. Even if she makes me feel more comfortable than I've ever been, it doesn't mean anything. She's probably able to make anyone feel special.*

Eun rubbed her chest and willed her foolish heart to get its act together and let her libido do what it wanted. She unzipped the side of her bag and took out her pajamas and toiletries bag. Shower, sex, and sleep were all she needed right now. And that was the lie she kept telling herself as she wiped her eyes while she brushed her teeth.

*

Morgan closed the door and locked it for the night. Rudy sat and waited for his leash to be removed. After filling his water bowl Morgan walked toward the sound of the shower. The bathroom door was open and through the white shower curtain she could see the outline of Eun's curvy body.

She tapped on the doorframe. "Okay to come in?"

Eun peeked around the shower curtain. "Suit yourself." She ducked back behind the plastic sheet.

Morgan grimaced at Eun's lukewarm invitation. "I don't know what to do, Eun."

"I know. I don't either. They left this out of the relationship handbook."

Morgan pulled her T-shirt over her head and dropped it to the floor. "There's a handbook?"

Through the curtain, Eun's breasts shimmied as she washed her hair. Morgan stripped off the rest of her clothes. With two fingers she pulled the curtain back and stepped into the tub. Eun turned to her and lowered her hands palm out. "Didn't you get yours with the toaster oven?"

Morgan laughed. "Anyone ever tell you you're funny?"

Eun quirked her mouth. "All the time. Everyone invites me to their parties so I can entertain."

Morgan moved closer. Eun shifted to the side of the tub to let her under the warm shower spray. Eun's hands moved over her shoulders and down to cup her breasts. "You are so beautiful, Morgan Wright." Eun bent her head and sucked Morgan's nipple into her mouth. Morgan gasped as she grazed her nipple with her teeth hard. She clasped Eun's shoulders. Her clit hardened and a raging fire of want settled between her legs.

Eun traced her fingers up the inside of Morgan's leg and brushed over her labia before she cupped her and squeezed. She slipped one finger in and stroked it gently in and out. Morgan widened her stance. Eun continued her fleeting touches, not enough to make Morgan come, but enough to make her want more. So much more.

Morgan panted as she teased her, fluttering her fingers over her clit. "I want you inside me, Eun."

Eun teased the wet seam between Morgan's legs. "Not here." She reached around Morgan and turned off the shower. "Bed."

"Bed." Morgan ripped the shower curtain open, popping one of the rings off in the process.

Eun stepped out of the tub and snagged a towel from the back of the door and dried herself before she passed it to Morgan.

Morgan rubbed the terrycloth over her skin impatiently before she tossed it on the sink. She leaned in and kissed Eun, slipping her hands under the wet strands of her hair. "Bed."

They clutched at each other as they bumped down the hall. At the door to Morgan's room they paused long enough for Morgan to flip the light switch to illuminate the bedside lamp. The bed was still rumpled from their before-dinner romp, the covers askew and half on the floor.

Eun turned them so Morgan's back was to the bed and walked her back until her calves hit the edge of the bed. She fell back and pulled Eun with her. Eun kissed her, her tongue tracing Morgan's lower lip. Morgan opened to her. Eun's hips ground into her and Morgan rocked up to meet her thrusts. Eun smoothed her hand over Morgan's stomach. Morgan shivered.

"You wanted me inside you?"

Morgan spread her legs wide. "Yes. Now. Don't tease."

Eun's fierce groan as she pushed inside Morgan rattled her chest where her body pressed against her.

"So good." Morgan closed her eyes.

"Look at me. Please." Eun's harsh whisper made Morgan open her eyes.

She held Eun's gaze.

Eun fucked her slowly, curling her fingers over the spot that made Morgan arch into her touch seeking more. "I want to watch you come." She sped her strokes up. "Give it up, Morgan, give me everything."

Morgan gasped and bucked her hips and Eun thrust deep and fast. She dug her fingers into Eun's hip. "Don't stop. Don't stop. Please."

"Never." Eun flicked her thumb over Morgan's clit and Morgan's body curled into Eun's strokes and she shouted as she came, captivated by the dark depths of Eun's eyes.

*

Morgan's body undulated like a wave when she came, and Eun locked her gaze on the golden-brown depths of her eyes. She clenched around Eun's fingers. Eun stilled and savored the sensation of Morgan's body drawing her fingers deeper.

She watched Morgan's face as she surrendered to her, a gift, one Eun would treasure. So many strong women hated to give it up, couldn't surrender control, couldn't trust another person to keep them safe in their most vulnerable moment. But Morgan did. She trusted Eun. Eun sensed it. Saw it. Believed it. Unable to tolerate the truth of Morgan's feelings, she closed her eyes. How was she going to give this up? How could life ever be the same after Morgan?

Morgan brushed damp strands of hair off her face. "You okay?"

Eun leaned down and kissed her gently and eased her fingers from Morgan. "Yes. You?"

"I've never come like that before." Morgan looked away from Eun.

Eun nuzzled her jaw. "Is it a bad thing? Did you enjoy it?"

"Yes. I mean, obviously." Morgan shifted from under Eun and they lay facing each other. "It was different."

Eun rubbed her thumb over Morgan's lower lip. "Don't you like it when you make someone come? When you know you're the one giving them pleasure and all they can do is take it? Knowing you're their whole world and focus? The awareness when they come, their body drawing you deeper, don't you feel it in your body and soul? The sensation of power? Why wouldn't I want to feel that way?"

Morgan's mouth lifted in a half smile. "I never thought of it like that."

Eun tugged Morgan over her and wrapped her legs around her narrow hips. "Now. Your turn. Make me forget my name and everything else in the world but you."

Morgan rotated her hips in a slow drag. "You like to play with toys?"

Eun lifted an eyebrow. "What did you have in mind?"

Morgan kissed her jaw and licked a line to the tender skin under her ear. "You like being fucked, right?"

Eun rocked her hips into Morgan. "You know the answer to that."

Morgan chuckled low. "I do. If you let me loose a minute, I'll get something we'll both enjoy."

Morgan leaned over the side of the bed. Her ass was perfection and Eun couldn't stop herself from sliding her hand over the smooth curve that led up to her back.

The snap of a drawer opening and the rustle of fabric as Morgan tossed a black nylon bag on to the bed sent a bolt of anticipation through Eun. She sat up and opened the drawstrings and poured out the contents on to the bed. A dildo fitted into a leather harness, a bullet vibrator, a pair of handcuffs, a small butt plug, condoms, and a large bottle of lube spilled over the bed.

Eun leaned on one elbow as she surveyed Morgan's collection. "What a naughty woman you are." She picked up the handcuffs and let them dangle off her fingers. "You like to be restrained? Or do the restraining?"

Morgan's bright gaze settled on her face. "I'm usually the top."

Eun sat up and leaned up on all fours. "That is not an answer."

Morgan kissed her back. "I haven't tried it. No one's ever asked me before. See anything you want to play with?"

Eun let the cuffs fall back to the bed. She picked up the dildo and harness. She stroked her hand over the thick shaft. "This." She tossed the toy to Morgan.

Morgan stood up and tugged the harness over her hips and tightened the straps into place. She tore open a condom and rolled it over the toy. Eun scooted to the edge of the bed and lay back. She spread her legs wide. She dipped her fingers into the liquid heat between her legs and gathered it on her fingers. "Not sure we'll need lube."

Morgan picked up the bottle and dribbled a small pool in her hand before she slicked the rampant toy. "Better safe than having to stop for some."

"True." Eun drew her feet up, her heels next to her ass cheeks, and let her knees drift wide. She held Morgan's gaze as she stroked herself. "Want any of this?"

Morgan's mouth quirked up on one side. "All of it." She lowered herself to her knees. She covered Eun with her mouth, her tongue sliding over Eun's hard clit as she pushed two fingers inside and spread them wide. Eun clasped her ankles and let her knees rest on the bed. Morgan licked her softly, and her deep sounds of appreciation and pleasure filled the room.

She rose and set the tip of the toy before she pushed slowly forward, filling Eun until she was flush against her. The leather of the harness brushed against the trimmed hair of Eun's core.

Eun raised her arms over her head and clasped her hands together. "Like this? You'd like it if I was cuffed to your bed and you could pleasure me however you wanted, wouldn't you?"

"Yes." Morgan rasped as she pulled back nearly to the tip and filled Eun again slowly. She rested her thumb on top of the hood of Eun's clit and rotated it in small circles.

"Do it. Do what you want, Morgan. Take all of it. Of me. I'm yours tonight."

Morgan inhaled sharply. "Don't say it if you don't mean it."

Eun held her gaze. "I don't say things I don't mean, Morgan."

Morgan closed her eyes for a moment. When she opened them, they blazed with a fire Eun had not seen before in her careful gentle lover. "Hold on."

Eun clasped her hands over her head. Morgan latched on to her hips, raised her up, and then pounded into her. The harsh drag and slide of each stroke hit all the right spots. Eun closed her eyes against the sharp waves of pleasure spiraling out from her center.

"Open your eyes." Morgan's low command washed over Eun.

She blinked her eyes open.

"No hiding." Morgan slowed her thrusts, drawing out Eun's pleasure. She rocked back into her hard.

Eun groaned and wet her lips. "That feels so fucking good."

Morgan rolled her hips, and the toy hit all new places inside, building a burning ache low in Eun's belly. "Finish me. I want to come."

Morgan pulled back, slid deep again, and then sped up. She changed her angle again, and Eun came with a shout. She curled her body and grabbed Morgan's shoulders. Eun clung to her as her body trembled and shook with pleasure.

Morgan placed her hands under her hips and lifted and pushed until they were lying on the bed. She braced herself on her arms and rocked into Eun gently. Another wave of pleasure washed over Eun, pulling her under and taking her breath away. Eun panted and held tight as she shuddered through the drawn-out orgasm that rolled over her. Morgan kissed her neck, her cheek, her mouth as slow aftershocks roiled her body.

Morgan shifted her hips and the toy slid gently from Eun's body. "Turn away from me on your side." Eun rolled to her side. Morgan lifted her leg and pulled it back over her hip and moved close to Eun. She entered her from behind and smoothed her hand down Eun's belly. Eun wiggled her ass back into Morgan. Morgan pressed her fingers lower and stroked her clit in tight circles as she rocked into Eun from behind. With each slow stroke the tip of the toy rubbed her sweet spot and Eun groaned with the sensation. "I don't know if I can come again."

"Only one way to find out." Morgan kept up her attentions on Eun's clit and matched them with her slow thrusts. Eun clung to Morgan's arm as she built a seething fire inside her.

Eun dug her nails into Morgan's forearm as she trembled through another bone-rattling orgasm. "Enough." She panted, her mind awash in pleasure. She closed her eyes and floated on the sensation of being wrapped in Morgan's arms. They stayed intertwined, enmeshed, until the last of Eun's pleasure ebbed away.

Morgan cupped her gently as she pulled free of her body and rolled over and away from Eun. The mattress shifted and Eun's skin was cool where Morgan had been. Eyes closed, she waited, listening to the clink of metal and the sounds of the toy being removed. And then Morgan was back, her warm hands caressing her body. She drew Eun in her arms and touched her everywhere, breasts, hips, her ass, branding her with her touch. She pressed her face into the crook of Morgan's neck and relaxed into her attention. Concerns about tomorrow and their future together floated away on a sea of bliss.

Chapter Fourteen

"Nice to see you again, Miss Park. This shouldn't take too long." The executor, Judy Mossberg, held out her hand.

Eun shook hands. "Thank you for handling this so quickly."

"Your father was very meticulous in his estate." Judy frowned. "Your uncle made noises like he wanted to challenge his will." She pushed her glasses up on her nose. "I assured him he would be wasting his time and money challenging it. Your father placed all his assets in a trust for you. It shelters you from taxes and is basically bulletproof to challenges. Your uncle can't touch anything. I need your signature on a few documents, and then I will file it with the clerk of courts."

She passed a large stack of documents to Eun. "I trust you had a chance to read over what I sent you. Will you want to read over them again before you sign?" She handed a thick black pen to Eun. "Would you like some coffee?"

"I'd like to review this again. I was a bit distracted when I was reading them in the hotel room."

"Would you like some coffee?"

"Coffee would be great." Eun took the documents and folded back the first cover sheet.

"Cream? Sugar?"

"No, thank you."

Judy left the room and returned with a paper cup filled with coffee. She placed it in front of Eun. "I'll leave you to it. My office is the first one on the left if you have any questions."

The quiet tick of the electric clock on the wall was loud in the stillness of the conference room. Eun sipped her coffee as she read over the documents.

After half an hour, Judy returned. "Any questions?"

"It looks all in order." Eun picked up the black pen to sign the documents. She worked her way through the pink sticky tabs marking each place she needed to sign. She signed her name on the final line. "Done." She capped the pen.

The sound of a strident voice from the next room spilled over into the conference room.

Eun grit her teeth as she listened to her uncle harangue Judy's office assistant, insisting he be let into the conference room.

Judy raised her eyebrow. "I thought we could avoid this by meeting early."

Eun pursed her lips. "My uncle is a force of nature. It's like trying to avoid an earthquake." She pinched her nose. "It's okay. Did my father leave anything to him?"

The executor held up a folder. "Not as much as he thought he was getting. Your father left him some cash."

Eun drummed her fingers on the table. "Any chance there's another way out of here?"

Judy pressed her lips together. "I'm sorry. No."

The door to the conference room banged open.

Uncle Max strode into the room. "What is going on in here?"

Eun spun the pen on the table and fixed her uncle with a glare and waited. *Don't talk. Wait.*

Judy squared her shoulders and straightened her posture. "We were, Mister Park, in the midst of finalizing the documents from your brother's estate."

"Stealing it. Stealing what was mine." The pitch of her uncle's voice climbed higher. "He promised me. He told me the house was mine. Better it burns to the ground than you have it. He would have burned it himself if he thought you'd foul it with your sickening lifestyle."

Eun clenched her jaw and stood. She faced away from her uncle and slid the documents toward Judy. "I take it you'll file this tomorrow?"

Her uncle made to snatch the documents from Eun. She stepped closer to Judy and placed them safely into her hands.

Judy raised her chin and clutched the papers to her chest with both hands as she glared at Eun's uncle. "Sir, if you don't calm down and act like a reasonable adult, I will have you removed from my office."

"Have me removed? She's the thief. And you are helping her. I will report you to the bar."

"You are free to do whatever you want. But if you want to pick up the check I have for you, you will sit down and be quiet."

Eun's uncle plopped into the chair at the opposite end of the conference room and placed his briefcase under the table. He looked down at his hands, his face twisted in silent rage.

Eun took advantage of his distraction and slipped out of the room. Greed would keep her uncle occupied for a few more minutes. She took her phone out and glanced at the time. She needed to make a quick visit to her father's house to ensure it was ready for the realtor to show. And then Morgan. Plenty of time for a going away lunch and maybe a little more.

*

The call from Eun's office came as she made the turn on to the street with Morgan's shop. She pulled over and parked across the street from Morgan's building to take the call. "Eunice Park."

Heather's was voice was clipped. "Eunice. Glad I caught you. I tried earlier but I got the 'do not disturb' message."

"I was at the executor's office signing the trust papers." The short hairs on Eun's neck stood up. "I'm on my way back today. I'll be at the office tomorrow."

"Don't bother. We've made some decisions while you've been gone. We're reorganizing the office to match the vision we have going forward. And we've decided you're no longer needed."

"What?" Eun's pulse rate sped up. "I'm sorry, what did you say?"

"We no longer require your services. We are not renewing your contract. We'll make sure you are compensated for the work you've done to date and anything else you have due."

Eun's breath caught in her throat, and her chest was tight.

"Eunice? Are you there?"

"Um, yes." She gripped the steering wheel with one hand, her knuckles white.

"We'll pack up your office up. No need for you to rush back now. We'll have everything delivered wherever you want us to send it. Would you drop your security badge in the mail?"

No words. She had no words. Her whole life since law school had been tied to the firm. All the hours she had worked, all the time she had given up, everything she had counted on, and after one short phone call, it was over. She pushed her hair back and dug her fingers into her scalp. Her father's words about not trusting anyone but yourself in business as he chided her for not opening her own practice echoed in her mind. She had spent her life building someone else's business, tying her dreams to a firm that had never appreciated her abilities. Her vision narrowed as her rage built.

"Yes. Of course." Her voice was hollow. The veneer of politeness she managed to keep in place strained her throat.

"Best of luck, Eunice."

The soft click of the disconnect rang in her head. She lowered her phone into her lap. Her knuckles ached, white where she gripped the steering wheel. "What the fuck? What the ever-living fuck?" Eun tossed the phone onto the seat. She banged both her hands on the car's steering wheel. "Fifteen fucking years and now I'm not needed? Fuck me."

She pinched the bridge of her nose hard, fighting against the fury filling her. Eun pounded the steering wheel again as she contemplated driving the six hours back to her office to punch Heather in her face before she set fire to the building.

*

Morgan glanced out of her window. Eun's car was parked across the street. Her head was resting on the steering wheel. Morgan leaned her head against the window mirroring her position. *What's she thinking? Why is she sitting there? Trying to decide if she should text me? Trying to figure out how to tell me goodbye? Have one last session of bone-melting sex?*

Morgan thumbed her phone on and pressed Eun's number. The phone rang. Once, twice, three times. Morgan watched out of the window as Eun held her position. After ten rings, the call went to voicemail. Morgan hung up without leaving a message. She turned from the window, her unanswered call all the message she needed.

Eun had been clear. She had a job, a career she was dedicated to. Morgan rubbed her chest, the dull ache of a missed opportunity for more with Eun flaring into a steady burn. *Why did I let myself get attached? Why did I let myself imagine we had a future together?* The pressure and warmth of Rudy as he leaned against her leg drew her gaze to the dog's deep-brown eyes.

"I'm a silly woman, Rudy." She bent and scratched his head. A knock at the door set him scampering toward the kitchen barking and wagging his tail. Morgan shoved her phone into her pocket and followed him, happy for the distraction.

Morgan pulled the door wide. Rudy braced his legs on the screen door and barked, his tail wagging. Eun stood on the landing, her face void of emotion.

Morgan opened the door and Eun stepped inside.

"You okay?"

"No. I'm not." Eun raked her hair back with one hand. "I'm not okay at all."

Morgan waited, her hands opening and closing at her sides. As much as she wanted to rush to Eun and take her in her arms, she waited, unsure of what Eun wanted.

Eun pursed her lips. "I should have known. After the last case. I should have guessed they'd do something like this."

"Who?"

"My firm. Or I should say my previous employer. They've decided I'm not needed. That the lawyer I was working with is a better fit. Ha. Wait till he screws up again and doesn't have me to blame. I wasn't even there to defend myself from his lies. Fuck."

Morgan tucked her thumbs into her pockets. "So, what does that mean?"

"It means I don't have a job." Eun's harsh shout echoed in the small kitchen.

Morgan stepped back. "Sorry. I'm sorry."

Eun covered her mouth with both hands. "No, I'm sorry. So sorry, Morgan. I shouldn't yell at you. It's not your fault."

"Is it why you didn't answer my call?"

Eun studied the toes of her shoes. "I was calculating how much jail time I'd get for punching the lead partner of my former firm."

"You shouldn't punch anyone. It's never as cool as it seems in the movies and it hurts your hand."

Eun quirked her mouth. "What's on your agenda today? Do you have time for a late breakfast or early lunch?"

Morgan tilted her head toward Rudy. "We were headed to the dog park. I promised him." Rudy yipped on cue.

"Care for company?"

Morgan picked up her bill cap from the hat rack and settled in on her head. "I'd love for you to hang out with us."

*

The dog park was empty except for an older man and an ancient basset hound shuffling along with his nose to the ground. Eun sat on the bench. Her gaze settled on Morgan as she tossed a tennis ball for Rudy. The bright-yellow ball bounced high. Rudy rose up and caught it.

He ran a short lap around Morgan before he brought it back to her feet for her to throw again. His bark was loud as he urged her to throw it. The joy on both their faces made her stomach flip. Why? Why hadn't she been able to find someone like Morgan before this? Someone who would have known her as a capable woman, and not the hot mess she currently was. A harsh wave of grief cascaded over her, and her chest ached. She missed her dad, the dad she had known before she came out, the father who made her feel smart and worthy of his love. How could he put her out of his life if he loved her?

Her mind struggled to reconcile the man who had been so proud of her, who had encouraged her, to the one who had shunned her. Her mind twisted back on itself as a Möbius strip of memories replayed in her mind. The image of her mother's face and her reluctance to sit with Eun at the funeral filled her vision. She snorted. Her mother was still unable to provide basic support, as able to abandon Eun as she had when she was a child.

Eun shivered in spite of the warm sun on her shoulders. As a child, Eun had wondered what she had done to make her mother leave her behind. When her father had rejected her, too, she wondered if she was too much, too much for anyone to love, because if your own parents didn't, or couldn't love you, who could?

Eun swallowed on the dry ache in her throat. Was she so easy to walk away from? Her first girlfriend had thought so, leaving Eun while she was on a business trip. Eun gripped her arms and dug her nails in to ground herself against the pain of remembering coming home to an empty apartment. As painful as it had been, it was marginally less painful than the Christmas party where she walked in on her second lover banging the senior partner from a rival law firm on Eun's desk.

In the years since, she had relied on the internet for quick hookups when she couldn't stand being alone anymore, desperate to remind herself of what it was like to be wanted. She had spent years avoiding relationships because she never wanted to feel that pain again.

She had held on to hope the first few years after she came out to her father, waiting for him to work through his issues. Eun had believed he would come around, that his love for her would finally win in the end. After the night she had come home to visit to find a group of his church friends ready to lay hands on her and pray away the gay, she had snapped, told them all to go to hell.

A harsh memory of screaming at him, shouting that if he couldn't accept her as she was, she was out of his life. His answering shouts, declaring he had no daughter, still haunted her. Five years. And then his call. She was haunted by the longing in his voice. And now he was gone, and they would never have the chance to settle things between them.

Eun leaned back against the wooden bench and closed her eyes as a thousand thoughts and memories spilled down her cheeks. A raging river of grief swallowed her whole as bone-deep sorrow engulfed her. Her body shook, and she tried to stifle her sobs.

Morgan's strong arms settled around her shoulders, and she let herself be pulled into a hug. The press and warmth of Rudy as he leaned against her legs, as Morgan held her, made her sob harder. A kaleidoscope of emotions raged through her, a violent carousel, a Tilt-A-

Whirl of feelings. A wave of nausea cramped her stomach. Her future spun out ahead of her, and she had no clue where it would lead. She knew right now she only wanted it to lead to Morgan's steady energy and the sweet dog that lay against her calves.

*

Morgan rubbed Eun's back in slow circles. Her body shook with silent sobs. Morgan held her close. Rudy jumped up on the bench and curled up next to Eun. He laid his muzzle over her thigh. Eun lifted her head, her face wet with tears and snot, and shifted to lean back on the bench. She stroked Rudy's head.

Morgan pulled a pack of tissues from her jacket pocket, took several from the pack, and passed them to Eun.

Eun took the tissues and looked away from Morgan's eyes as she wiped her face and blew her nose. "Sorry." Her voice was thick and phlegmy.

"For what? I'm thinking that was long overdue." Morgan sat back on the bench and rolled the tennis ball along her thigh.

Eun twisted the tissue in her hands. "I haven't cried much. It hurt too bad. I was worried if I started, I'd never stop. I cried every day for months when my mom left us."

Morgan held Eun's gaze and waited for her to continue, sensing she had more to say.

"I kept thinking she would come back. If I was good enough."

"No. That was all on your mom, Eun. You were a kid. It had nothing to do with you."

Eun picked at the fabric of her suit coat. "I know that. I know that now. But then I didn't. Addiction is a terrible thing. And my dad fixed it so she could never see me even if she wanted to."

Morgan pursed her lips. "That's harsh."

Eun sighed. "I think he thought he was protecting me."

Morgan rubbed the back of her neck. "Parents do a lot of wacky stuff sometimes, out of love."

Eun wiped at her face again. "He hated I was lesbian. Hated it. Hated me."

Morgan grabbed Eun's hand. "I'm sorry. But did he really hate you? Or was he mad you weren't like he wanted you to be? Mad you fell off the perfect plan he had laid out for you. It's hard on parents when kids don't do what you want, when they make their own decisions."

"I was the perfect child. Valedictorian in high school. Top of my class in college and law school. I did everything out of fear he would abandon me, thinking if I was perfect enough, I could make him happy. He really loved my mom. It destroyed him she chose drugs over us. He never got over it. He became uber Christian afterwards. My uncle is big into it, and it became my dad's drug. He was as hooked on it as my mom was on Percocet. We were at church every time it was open—Sundays, Wednesdays, Fridays. I think he thought going to church would keep me from following my mom's path." Eun shivered. "I don't know what I'm going to do without a job."

Morgan stood. Rudy lifted his head and jumped off the bench. Morgan snapped his leash on before she held out her hand to Eun. "Come on. You don't have to decide right now. Let's get something to eat. You can't drive back to Chicago. You're too wrung out."

Eun lifted her shoulders and let them fall. "I can take my time now. Not like I have to rush back to the office."

"Come on, I have a craving for Mai's Gyeran-jjim."

Eun rolled her eyes. "Are you always hungry?"

Morgan laughed. "More often than not."

Eun took her hand and tugged her close. She pressed a gentle kiss to Morgan's cheek. "Sorry I dumped all my family stuff on you."

Morgan curled her arm around Eun's shoulders. "It's fine. Every family has its stuff."

Eun leaned against her. "How were your folks when you came out?

"Not surprised about me. Not really. Miesha was kind of a surprise. Neil being pan was the biggest surprise.

"Wait, what? All of you?"

"Yep. All of us. My mom struggled a bit, but my uncle's gay, and my dad had worked through his feelings, plus he saw how hard it was on my uncle when my grandparents were unsupportive. My dad didn't want us to feel like his brother ever."

Eun rested her arm around Morgan's waist and leaned her head against her shoulder. "I can't even imagine what that would be like. My dad lost his mind. Cut me off, demanded I pay him back for law school. It pissed him off when I paid him back and added a bit, to fuck with him, to prove his predictions about my success were way off the mark."

The truck chirped when Morgan unlocked it. She lifted Rudy up and placed him in the back of the crew cab and buckled his harness into his seatbelt.

"You have a seatbelt for him?"

"Well, yeah, dogs need them too. It keeps him from trying to ride in my lap. And safe if we had an accident."

Eun raised an eyebrow. "Do you want kids? You'd be a great parent."

"What? Is this a test? I'm not prepared."

Eun's hearty laugh made Morgan determined to hear it again.

After fastening her seatbelt, Morgan started the truck. "Where to?"

"You said we could get Gyeran-jjim."

"Eggsellent."

Eun groaned at Morgan's silliness. "That was terrible."

Morgan pulled out of the parking lot and onto the blacktop leading back to town. "If you're tired and don't want to stay at your dad's house because it's too weird, you're welcome to crash at my place. You could drive back tomorrow when you're rested."

Eun rested her palm on Morgan's thigh. "Thank you. But I'm fine to drive back. I need to get back and find a job."

"Will money be an issue? Are you going to be okay?"

Eun drummed her fingers on the seat. "Yeah. I've never had enough time to spend what I make. My colleagues used to tease me about being tight with money. But after I paid my dad back, saving most of my money was a habit. I don't carry debt. My condo and car are paid for. With what my dad left plus what I'll get from the house I could take a couple of years off if I wanted to."

"That's good. Debt sucks. It keeps you stuck. What would be so bad about taking some time off?"

"Trying to get rehired after that would be a nightmare."

Morgan piloted the truck down the street to her house.

"I'll be all right, Morgan. Both to drive home and after. It's not that far. And the realtor will have the house listed in a few weeks." Eun pushed her hair back with both hands. "Ginny is doing a great job with getting the office cleaned out. I can't even begin to make sense of what he was working on. It's all jumbled. So unlike my dad. He was always so organized."

Morgan pursed her lips. "Maybe he was tired of being perfect?"

"Maybe. But something's off. I can't put my finger on it. Ginny has been a lifesaver."

"Why didn't you open your own practice?"

Eun huffed out a breath. "My father asked me that for years."

"Sorry. We don't have to talk about it." Morgan glanced in the rearview mirror and then back at the road.

"It's okay. I didn't want the hassle. I wanted the prestige of working for a big firm. My dad always gave me a hard time for making money for other people." Her fingers tightened on Morgan's thigh. "He was right. Damn it. I spent years with my firm. I made them a fuck ton of money and now they ditch me for a snot-nosed kid who doesn't know his ass from a hole in the ground."

"Their loss."

Eun shifted in her seat. "I wish I didn't care so much. I've never failed at anything in my life. Well, other than relationships."

"I wouldn't call them firing you a failure. I'd call it misguided on their part. From what you've told me it's pretty cutthroat at your office anyway, right?"

"Right. And what gets me is, I should have hired a company to clean everything out and sold the place. I should have left after the funeral." Eun looked away from Morgan. "I let myself get distracted, and he was there the whole time, poisoning them against me. I bet the little pig even blamed me for the case we lost right before I left. So close to making partner. I took my eyes off the prize. So stupid of me. I've got to get back and see where I can land."

Morgan bit her lip. The sting of Eun's dismissing their time together as a distraction, as something she regretted, soured her stomach. She parked the truck in back of her apartment. "Wait here. I'll run him up."

She threw open the truck door, slammed it shut, and then opened the passenger side door to unfasten Rudy's seatbelt. He licked the side of her face as she leaned in to attach his leash. She lifted him out and hugged him to her chest before she placed him on the ground. At least she'd get the dog after all.

Chapter Fifteen

Eun scowled at the bright-red and yellow balloons tied to the mailbox in front of a low brick house three doors down from her father's house. She rolled her eyes at the minivan parked in front of the hydrant across the street from her father's house. Summoning her best parking skills, she wedged her car into a tight parallel space on the narrow residential street. After she shut the engine off, Eun shoved the door open. Cars lined both sides of the street as far as she could see.

Eun considered leaving a rude note on the windshield of the pickup truck blocking the driveway to her father's house. After a minute of searching in her handbag for paper, she gave up on the idea and stalked down the driveway. The scrape of her shoes on the concrete added to her annoyance.

The day had been a slow-moving train wreck. Lunch with Morgan had been a spectacular disaster. Morgan's sudden distance was disconcerting and confusing and their awkward goodbye left Eun more certain than ever she was destined to be alone for the rest of her life.

Returning to Chicago was the right thing to do. She had to get her life back together, she didn't have the time or energy for a relationship. Not now. Maybe not ever. And it was fine. It was easier to work without distractions anyway. Even if the distraction was a woman whose smile lit Eun up from the inside. Morgan was a beautiful soul, and Eun already regretted not leaving it better with her.

She chewed her lip and wished she were on the highway back to Chicago with her memories of Sikesville tightly stuffed and sealed into the recesses of her memory. Eun huffed out a breath and chastised herself again for forgetting the packet from her father's executor on the kitchen counter. She cursed quietly as she walked and dug through her purse for the house keys as she navigated the sidewalk to her father's house.

Her cavernous purse refused to release the keys. Eun paused and bent over her bag. She swore as she shook the bag, desperate to pick up the papers and make her escape from Sikesville. The acrid smell of smoke stung her nose as her fingers closed over the ring of keys. Triumphant, Eun straightened before she glanced up at the house.

Wisps of smoke seeped from under the eaves of the house and drifted across the sky. She clutched the keys so hard they dug into her palm. Her hands trembled as she pulled her phone from her bag. It slipped from her sweaty hands and hit the driveway.

"Fuck. No, no, no." Eun dropped to her knees, ignoring the pain of the rough concrete. She snatched the phone up. The screen was cracked. *Please let it work. Please.*

White smoke billowed from the house slowly before it morphed and then became a torrent of dark gray. Eun pressed the home button and the screen lit up. She dialed 9-1-1. The operator picked up on the first ring.

"Nine-one-one, what is your emergency?"

"I'm at nine twenty-three Baker Street and it's on fire."

"Get out of the house. Do not go back in. Go to a safe spot away from the house. Wait across the street for assistance."

"Got it." Eun glanced down the crowded suburban street before she crossed to the other side. She hugged her purse close to her body. The smoke gathered under the eaves of the roof. Eun clenched and unclenched her hands as she waited. The smoke became black and thick.

The sound of distant sirens approaching sent her already racing heart rate into overdrive. A fire truck navigated the car-lined street. Eun lifted her hand to flag them down. The ladder truck pulled up in between the rows of parked cars. A smaller car with a siren on top arrived from the other direction.

A firefighter approached Eun. "Are you the one who called?"

"Yes. I'm Eunice Park." Eun gestured at the house. "It was smoking when I arrived."

"Anyone inside?"

"No." Eun wrapped her arms around herself tightly.

The firefighter turned and spoke into her radio. Firefighters in turnout gear swarmed from the truck and surrounded the house. A dull roar filled Eun's ears. She bent at the waist and breathed into her hands.

The firefighter beside her continued to give orders. Eun tuned out the rest of the conversation. Her knees buckled, and she leaned against the hood of her car as another fire truck arrived and firefighters swarmed the scene. They pulled hoses from the fire trucks and tugged them into place. A crash sounded as the windows were broken out of the minivan parked in front of the hydrant and a hose dragged through it. Neighbors began to gather in their yards.

A sensation of detachment settled over her as she watched the firefighters battle the blaze as it spread across the roof. The world narrowed to the scene before her. A gaping maw opened in the roof. Flames and smoke shot skyward. Eun gasped when the roof collapsed and sent up a shower of sparks. Her stomach churned. Eun swallowed the bile in her throat.

"Eunice! Are you all right? Were you inside?" The overly concerned voice of Ginny Burns's husband, Adam, startled Eun.

"I'm fine." Eun lifted her chin and lied. Her chest was tight. Her heart stuttered as the firefighters hosed down what was left of her family home.

Adam's brow was covered in a fine sweat. The sheen on his brow made Eun grimace. He clasped her arm. "You could have been killed. My cousin died when her house went up. She was trapped when it flashed over." He wiped a hand over his forehead before he pressed his hand to his chest. "The lord is merciful."

Eun pulled her arm free and squinted at him. "What are you doing here?"

He rubbed his fingers over his lips "What? Oh. Ginny forgot...her Bible on the desk in the office. I came to pick it up for her."

The hairs on Eun's neck raised at his hesitation. Too many years of taking depositions for her to let the bald-faced lie go. "Now? Seems an odd time."

He flushed. "She wanted it for Bible study tomorrow. Got to run now. I take it she won't need to come to work?"

"No. I'll call her when I figure out what to do." Eun cocked her head to the side. The lead firefighter walked toward them.

"Gotta run." Adam inclined his head and hurried down the street away from the fire.

Eun's gut twisted. Adam's discomfort and sudden departure pricked at Eun's mind. *Where the hell was he parked? He didn't just arrive. And why didn't I see him before?*

"Miss Park, I'm Captain Michaels with the Sikesville Fire Department. I need to get some information from you."

"Yes, of course."

"Are you feeling okay? We could sit in my car if you want to rest a bit."

"I'd rather get this over with." Eun fiddled with her purse strap.

"I understand. I'm sorry. Fires are frightening and can be devastating to the family. Do you have somewhere to stay?"

"I was on my way back to Chicago, and yes, I have a place to stay for tonight."

"You told the officer in charge the structure was on fire when you arrived?

"Yes." Eun gestured the driveway. "I stopped to find the keys. I smelled something acrid, and there was smoke pouring out from under the eaves."

"Was there one spot that seemed to be smoking more?"

Eun frowned and pointed to the corner of the building housing her father's office. "It was heaviest at that corner. It spread out from there."

Captain Michaels noted Eun's answer on her clipboard. "What color was the smoke?"

"It was white and then turned a dark-gray, I think." Eun rubbed her forehead and struggled to focus as she answered the rest of the fire captain's questions. Her mind strayed back to Adam's sudden appearance and their odd interaction.

"That's all I need for now." Captain Michaels tucked her clipboard under her arm. She passed Eun her card. "If you have any questions or remember anything we haven't talked about, please call me."

"Thank you." Eun took the card and slid it into her bag.

"You sure you're settled as far as housing? Is there anyone you can call to stay with you?"

"I'm sure. And I'll be fine. Thank you for your concern." Eun set her teeth on her trembling lip. "I'm fine." Eun looked away from the expression of doubt on Captain Michaels' face.

*

Eun collapsed onto the fluffy white cover on the hotel bed. At least she'd been able to find a room. She kicked off her heels and slid up on the bed, tucking her hands behind her head. Inventory. That's what she needed to do. Make a column of what she had and what she didn't have. It was an exercise she had perfected in her years as a lead attorney.

A cold wave of resentment swept over her again. What was she going to do? Money was not an issue. But time on her hands was. What did people do who didn't work seventy-hour weeks? She rolled to her side. The red numbers on the bedside clock glared at her. She could call Morgan. But why? Their lunch had left a bad taste in Eun's mouth. Morgan had already written her off; that much was clear. She was done. An ache bloomed in Eun's chest.

Why was it so easy for people to walk away from her? And why hadn't she walked away first?

She picked up her phone and dialed the only person she could.

Roslyn answered on the first ring. "Hey, when are you coming home?"

"Hello, and I don't know. I was going to be there late tonight but there was a fire at my dad's house. And Heather fired me."

"What?" Roslyn screeched into the phone. "Wait, a fire? Are you all right? How bad was it? And how can she do that? Don't you have a contract?"

"I'm okay. I wasn't home when the fire started." Eun inhaled through her nose and then huffed out a breath. "And Heather's not renewing my contract. She's going to pay me out."

"Geez, honey, I'm sorry. Are you going to be okay, money wise?

"Yeah. That's not an issue. At least for right now."

"Do you need me to come?"

"Can you? I feel like I'm losing my mind."

"I'll be there tomorrow. And why wouldn't you? Lost your dad, lost your job, and a fire. Why wouldn't you be a mess?"

"Getting fired was bad enough, but it was awful watching my dad's house burn." Eun swallowed around the dry ache in her throat. "Even if I hadn't lived there for years. It was still my home."

"I'm so sorry, baby. I'll be there tomorrow by noon."

"Thanks, Roz."

"Hug yourself tight. See you for lunch.

"Hug Jeff and Julie for me." Eun thumbed the call off and placed the phone on her nightstand.

Forcing herself out of bed, she made her way to the bathroom and spun the tap to fill the tub. She rummaged through the offered assortment of hotel toiletries. After selecting a lemon-scented bath oil, she dumped it into the tub. Eun piled a stack of towels on the counter before she stripped and stepped into the water. The tub was standard hotel issue, and she had to bend her knees to fit into it. She let the water get as high as she dared before she shut it off.

The porcelain was cold on her skin when she leaned against the back of the tub. She closed her eyes. Visons of the fire flooded her thoughts and she opened her eyes. She hugged her knees to her chest. A thousand what-ifs swirled in her mind as she imagined what would have happened if she had not noticed the smoke and opened the door. A shiver slid through her. *I'm alive. And here. And that's all that matters, isn't it? But here for what? No family to speak of. No one in my life except for Roz who cares for me. Hell, even Mom couldn't be bothered to stick around.*

Using both hands, she splashed water over her face. Morgan had acted like she cared, until she didn't. Why? Because Eun chose to go back to her life? Mentally, Eun reviewed their talk at the dog park. And then it hit her. She had said coming to Sikesville was a mistake. And Morgan was part of Sikesville. A big part. She had gone out of her way to help Eun, over and over again, without asking for anything. And Eun had said it was a mistake.

Eun stood and water slopped over the side of the tub. She wrapped a towel around her and padded into the room, not caring she dripped on the floor. She tapped her cracked phone screen and pressed Morgan's number. She nibbled her thumb as it rang. And rang. And rang. When the voicemail answered Eun hung up, not even knowing where to begin to explain. If she called now Morgan would see it as Eun, once again, only reaching out when she needed something from Morgan.

In the bathroom she dropped the towel to the floor before she stepped back into the tub. The soft lemon scent and warm water failed to wash away the stubborn ache in her heart. She lay back and smoothed her fingers over her body. Her nipples peaked in the cool air, and she sunk lower in the tub and the warmth.

Desperate for distraction, she cupped her breasts and rolled her nipples. The zing of sensation sent a bit of pleasure to her clit. With both hands she rolled her nipples, savoring the sensations, imagining Morgan's hands were where hers were. The confines of the tub frustrated her, and she unplugged it, dried herself briskly, and dug through her toiletry bag for the small vibrator she always carried on her trips.

In the room, she pulled back the covers and slid between the sheets, the crisp fabric cool against her warm skin. She turned the vibrator on, the low hum muffled by the covers, and closed her eyes. Visions of Morgan and her body over Eun's merged with sense memories of the way she reverently touched Eun, like she was precious and worthy and desirable. More than a quick fuck. Eun had seen in her eyes how much more she wanted. She touched the tip of the vibrator to her clit, a light touch, just enough to make her want more.

With the other hand she rolled her nipple, and then she pressed the vibrator hard against her clit. The slow vibe built a deep heat in her body, she edged herself, holding out until she couldn't. She curled up her shoulders, lifting from the bed as she came. She held the vibrator in place and caught the wave again, her orgasm slower and deeper this time. She turned it off and lay back. Her body throbbed with her orgasm. She curled on her side and pushed away the sensation of having lost something she had no right to want as tears slid down her face and wet the pillow as the ache of being alone wrapped itself around her heart.

Chapter Sixteen

Roslyn leaned forward in her seat. "This is a cute place. You made it sound like Sikesville was such a backwater."

"Things have changed a lot since I lived here."

Roslyn pursed her lips. "I can't believe that bitch fired you. What a heartless ass."

Eun sipped her tea. "I can't either. But it is what is."

"We've got space at my firm. My boss would scoop you up in a heartbeat."

Eun pulled her hand away and tucked it under her thigh. "Thank you. I know. I know I should leave."

"But?"

Eun met her gaze. "Morgan."

"The hottie you told me about?"

Eun grimaced. "Yes. I left it bad with her. I hate that. But I don't even know where to start to apologize. And even if I do, it's not like she'd leave here, and I'm sure as hell not staying. Not now. I don't even have a place to live."

Roslyn sat back in the booth. "So, come back. Let it go. Why bother? Let the insurance company work it out and then have it demolished. Sell the lot, easy-peasy."

Eun shoved her hair back with both hands. "I don't know if I can let go that easy."

"We're not talking about the house now, are we?"

"No." Eun covered her mouth with both hands.

"Good sex is hard to give up."

"It's not only the sex." At Roslyn's raised eyebrow she continued. "It's all of it. She is so open, honest. She's like standing in a cold shower until you can't take it anymore. No games. She's for real. I don't even know what to do with that kind of honesty. But I don't want to give it up. Not yet."

"So, don't. Apologize. Take some time to find out if it's as good as you think it is. You don't have to plunge right back into work. You've said you're good on money. Close your condo up, pack up your shit, and move here. Rent something and give it a go. You've done nothing but what everyone else has wanted you to do since you were a kid. Take some time for yourself." She leaned over the table. "The job will be there. I'm up for partner, and unless I kill someone between now and the next board meeting, I'm in. I'll always have space for you. Don't let that keep you from figuring out what you want to do. Take your time. Enjoy all the things you've missed being the perfect daughter."

Eun rolled her empty water glass between her hands. "Maybe you're right. They say not to make any big decisions for the first year after someone close to you dies."

"It's your time now, honey. Take advantage of it."

"Thanks, and thanks for coming. I didn't know who else to call."

Roz snorted. "You should call me more often. I could have come for the funeral, you know. And Jeff understands. And even if you stay, you need to come back for Julie's kindergarten graduation."

"I'll be there."

Roslyn reached out and took Eun's hand in both of hers. "I love you, Eun. Do what's best for you." Eun lifted her hand and kissed the back of it. "Love you too. And thank you."

A movement at the door caught Eun's attention. She recognized the set of the broad shoulders under the tan work shirt and her heart squeezed. Morgan. And she didn't even say hello? Because why would she? Eun had implied their relationship was a mistake. Time to fix it and make it right if she could.

*

After stopping by the post office to mail a package, Morgan turned left and walked the two blocks toward Ohana's. Her stomach grumbled. The two slices of raisin bread she had for breakfast were long gone. Morgan's mouth watered as she thought ahead to lunch. The restaurant was crowded with lunchtime guests. Morgan stood near the door waiting to be seated.

As she waited, she picked up the local newspaper and scanned the front page. Her eyes widened as she saw the reports of a fire and recognized Eun's father's house. A cold sweat broke out along her spine. A quick read of the article listed no injuries. The fire had happened the afternoon after their last lunch together. A picture of a distraught Eun standing next to Fire Captain Mel Michaels made Morgan clench her jaw. Eun hadn't even called Morgan. *Fucking house burns to the ground and she didn't even think to call me? What'd I expect after our goodbye, thanks-for-playing-and-the-sex-but-it-was-a-mistake-and-I'm-leaving lunch.* Morgan traced her fingers over the photograph. And now she knew for certain where their budding relationship was going. Which was nowhere.

She tossed the paper aside and studied the toes of her workbooks. *What did I expect? She was never going to stay, no matter what. She made it clear from the beginning. Any thoughts I entertained about her staying was a silly fantasy. Women like her never choose women like me, not for the long term. They choose women who wear slick power suits. Women who drive sporty cars, not diesel trucks, never women who get their hands dirty every day, even if they do own their own business.* She scuffed her boot on the rug. *Fuck me. What was I thinking?*

The unmistakable low timbre of Eun's voice caught Morgan's attention. She lifted her gaze and scanned the dining area. Eun was at a two top, sitting across from a woman Morgan didn't recognize. The woman reached out and held Eun's hand with so much tenderness, Morgan looked away from the intimate scene. *So much for going back to Chicago. Did she think in a town this size she could hide she was still here? Fuck. Why couldn't she say she didn't want to date me, or whatever we've been doing?* Her stomach flipped. She turned her back and left, the reality of Eun's rejection burning her skin.

*

The bundle of roses clenched in Eun's fist dripped water over her fingers. Eun shifted the bouquet to her left hand and wiped her wet palm on her pants. She knocked on Morgan's door. Rudy's sharp bark echoed in the hallway.

Eun took a half step back from the door. She waited. Nothing. No call for Rudy to stop barking. She pressed her face against the door and rested her palm on the painted wood door. "Easy, Rudy. It's me." The barking shifted to whining and scratching. Desperate to see Morgan, tired of her texts and calls being unreturned, Eun had taken a chance on finding her at home.

What to do? Leave the flowers? Leave a note? This is what I get for being spontaneous. Eun rubbed her forehead. A noise on the stairs behind her made her spin in its direction. Morgan walked up the steps toward her. Eun clutched the bouquet tighter.

Morgan's shirt was sweat-stained and dusty. A frown spoiled her face. "What are you doing here?" She stepped up on the landing and crossed her arms. Rudy barked and scratched the door.

"I wanted to say I'm sorry." Eun held out the flowers, her arm stiff.

Morgan squared her shoulders and jutted her jaw forward. "For which thing? Lying about going back to Chicago? Or your girlfriend? I'm nobody's side piece."

"What the hell are you talking about?" Eun rocked back on her heels as Morgan's anger spilled over the space between them.

"It's a small town, Eun. I saw you, with her."

"Back up. What are you talking about?"

"At Mai's." Morgan stepped past Eun and opened the door. Rudy ran out and circled Eun once and ran back in after Morgan.

Eun stood on the outside of the open door, unsure what to do. *That explains the unanswered texts. But what the fuck, she thinks so little of me she assumed I was lying? And a cheater?*

Morgan returned with Rudy on a leash. She brushed past Eun, not speaking as she led him down the stairs.

Eun's hand ached where she gripped the roses. She stormed down the steps after Morgan and followed her across the parking lot to a small group of trees and grass.

Morgan's face was a mask of stone. Rudy wandered around doing his business and sniffing the grass and bushes.

Eun waited until she had her anger under control before she spoke. She took a breath and kept her voice measured. "I'm not a liar, Morgan. That was my best friend, who, if you hadn't run out of the restaurant, I could have introduced you to. I intended to drive back to Chicago when I left after lunch. I stopped by my father's house to pick up some paperwork I had forgotten. There was a fire. You were so distant the last time we were together I didn't want to bother you that night. And then I did try, and you didn't return my calls and texts." At her continued silence, Eun looked away from Morgan. "If I had opened the door to my dad's house I could have been burned or killed. I could have died. I've spent the last three days in my hotel room trying to get myself together, to decide what to do."

Morgan crossed her arms and stared at Eun. "What to do? About what? Rudy? You going to take him with you?" Morgan's hands gripped the leash tighter.

"About us." Eun tilted her head and met Morgan's hard gaze. "I had decided to stay. To take some time to see where this, us, might lead. But if you're so fucking immature you jump to conclusions, refuse to answer my texts, and then stonewall instead of talking when I show up in person, maybe I need to stick to my original plan. Don't worry; he's yours. I wouldn't take him from you. I hope you'll be happy together."

Eun turned her back on Morgan. She dumped the roses into a trash bin and stalked away, ignoring Morgan's shouts as she climbed into her car. Gravel pinged against the side of the car as Eun gunned the engine and drove out of the parking lot. She chewed her lip, checked her gas gauge, took one last look in her rearview mirror, and turned toward the interstate.

*

The remote chirped as Morgan unlocked it on the run. She lifted Rudy into place and buckled him in before climbing in her seat. She hit call back on Eun's last text to her.

"What?"

"Where're you?"

"A gas station, and why do you want to know?"

"Because I want to talk to you."

"How is now any different than five minutes ago?"

"I'm sorry. Tell me where to be and I'm there."

Silence on the other end made Morgan pull the phone away from her face to see if they were still connected.

"Okay." Eun's voice was tired.

Morgan rubbed her chest. "Where do you want to meet?"

"I'll come to you." Eun disconnected the call.

Morgan turned the truck off. She leaned her forehead against the wheel. A sharp yip from Rudy made her look up. Mel Michaels stood outside her door.

Morgan opened the door and climbed out. "Hey, what's up?"

Mel peered into the truck. "You alone?"

"Yeah, well except for Rudy. Why?"

"Do you know where Eun is? I got a call from the fire investigator. I need to talk to her."

Morgan raised an eyebrow. "What?"

Mel crossed her arms. "I can't say anything to you, but do you know where she is? Miesha said you might know."

Eun's bright-red Mustang entered the parking lot and stopped next to Morgan's truck. The door swung open and Eun exited the car.

Mel stepped back and turned to face Eun. "Hi, Miss Park."

Eun grimaced. "Please call me Eun. To what do I owe the pleasure of seeing you again?"

Mel glanced at Morgan. "Could we go inside to talk?"

Morgan lifted Rudy from the back seat. "Sure."

Eun followed Morgan up the stairs to the apartment with Mel flanking them.

As soon as they were inside, Morgan closed the door and locked it.

Mel took a notebook from her pocket and flipped to a clean page. "Eun, do you have anyone with reason to harm you? Or threaten you?"

"What?"

Mel cocked her head to the side. "We found evidence of arson."

Eun's eyes widened. "No. I mean my uncle hates me, but I don't think he'd go as far as arson."

"Can you give me his contact information? Did he have keys to your father's house?"

"Yes. And I don't know. He and my father were close, but I don't know if he had keys."

"Can you account for your whereabouts prior to the fire?"

"What? You think I burned down a house I own? What the hell?"

"Sorry, I have to ask."

Morgan stepped forward and rested her palm on Eun's lower back. "She was with me."

Mel raised an eyebrow and flipped her notebook closed. "Are you planning on staying in town?"

Eun jutted her chin out. "I'm not sure."

"Will you let us know if you decide to leave town?"

"Officer, unless I am formally charged, my comings and goings are no concern of yours." Eun shifted away from Morgan's side and squared her body. "Any other conversations we might have will occur in the presence of my attorney."

Mel sighed and shoved her notepad back into her pocket. "Have it your way."

Morgan crossed her arms over her chest and watched the two women as they stared at each other. Marginally contained rage boiled off Eun's body and filled the kitchen.

Mel stepped back, lifted her chin toward Morgan. "See ya, Miss Park." She leaned down and scratched Rudy's head before she left.

Chapter Seventeen

Morgan locked the door behind Mel. Eun turned to watch her. She clasped her arms across her chest. *Wait. Let her speak first.*

Morgan rubbed the back of her neck. "Can we have a do-over?"

Eun tilted her head. "From what part? Where I showed up to apologize and you blew me off? Or when we met? Or what? What do you want, Morgan?"

Morgan crossed to Eun and took her in her arms. Eun held herself stiff, unwilling to let go of her anger just yet.

"You. I want you." Morgan kissed her, and Eun melted against her body. No words. Eun dug her fingers into Morgan's hips and pulled her tighter against her and took over the kiss. Raw hunger filled her, and she groaned into Morgan's mouth. How could she give this up?

Morgan broke their kiss. She held Eun close. "I'm sorry. I shouldn't have assumed."

Eun kissed the hollow of Morgan's throat and then nipped the salty skin there. Morgan hissed. Eun nipped her again, pushed her back. She yanked hard, and the snaps of Morgan's work shirt opened from top to bottom. "No, you shouldn't have."

"Sorry. Forgive me?."

Eun answered by kissing Morgan hard enough to bruise her lips.

Panting, Morgan stepped back and ripped her sports bra over her head and tossed it on the counter. She pushed Eun back against the refrigerator and ground against her and moved her hands to the hem of her shirt.

Eun groaned into her kiss. "I'm still furious." She dug her nails into Morgan's waist.

Morgan kissed her and nipped her lip. "I know." In one smooth motion Morgan stripped Eun's shirt off and dropped it on the counter. She lowered her head and mouthed and bit Eun's nipples through her bra. The heat of her mouth as she closed her lips over Eun's nipples sent a wicked current of desire through her.

Morgan reached up and unhooked the front hook of her bra. The lace cups opened, and Eun's breasts spilled free. Morgan laved her nipples with her tongue. Burning with desire, Eun pushed Morgan's shirt off her shoulders before she scraped her short nails over the nape of her neck.

Morgan lifted her head and her scalding gaze slid over Eun. "Take your pants off."

Eun met her gaze. "You do it."

"Turn around, hands on the table." Morgan rested her hands on her hips.

"Make me." She thrilled at taunting Morgan, ready for her sweet side to disappear into the harsh lover Eun craved. The need to surrender her control, to let Morgan take charge, to have one thing she could count on as her life spun out of control.

Morgan grabbed her hips and spun Eun so she faced the table. With one hand in the middle of her back, she pushed her flat and kept her pinned in place while she unhooked the top button of her pants. "Don't move." Morgan hooked her thumbs inside the waistband of Eun's pants. She lowered them to her ankles and drew them off, leaving Eun's sheer thong in place. She lay over her, gathered her wrists together in one hand, and stretched her hands over her head.

She pressed her breasts against Eun's back. The press of her skin made Eun crave more.

Morgan ground against her, the fabric of her jeans scraping Eun's skin. "You like it rough, don't you?" She bit the curve of Eun's shoulder and shifted her hips, rocking forward.

"See for yourself." Eun turned her head to the side, twisting to watch Morgan's expression.

Morgan shifted and drew her fingers over her ass before dipping down to her swollen center. She shoved her fingers under the damp fabric of the thong. Eun groaned and shifted her hips back, seeking contact.

Morgan teased a finger between her slick lips. Pressing inside, she slid her fingertips up and down, wetting them before she rubbed Eun's clit in slow circles. Eun panted as sensation rocketed through her. "Just fuck me."

Morgan drew her hand away and brought it down with a crack on Eun's ass. "No. Not until you ask nicely."

Eun struggled against Morgan's grip until she tightened it. She pressed her face to the cool wood of the table and relaxed into Morgan's control.

Morgan kissed her shoulder blades and rubbed Eun's ass, soothing where she had smacked her. "We should have settled this before now. Safe words?"

Eun wiggled her ass. "Red to stop. Yellow to slow down."

Morgan bit her shoulder. Eun groaned and rotated her hips. The dull ache and press of Morgan's teeth on her skin skittered over her, and her clit throbbed with the sensation of being had, taken, out of control.

"Got it. Do you like to cry?"

Eun bit her lip. "Sometimes." Her face burned with the acknowledgment of the side of herself she hid from other lovers. The part of her that craved a lover's control, her desire to relax into the sensations, to feel, to simply be in the moment.

Morgan kissed between her shoulder blades and ran her tongue over the spot she had bitten. "Keep your hands over your head." She released her grip on Eun's wrists. Moving behind Eun, she drew her thong down her legs. The soft skin of Morgan's face slid along her legs as Morgan nuzzled and nibbled her way from Eun's ankle to the crease under her ass cheek. "Spread your legs."

Eun knotted her hands together and widened her stance. The wood table legs squeaked on the floor.

Morgan's hands massaged her ass, pinching and squeezing her flesh. "I love your ass." She moved to the side and patted Eun's ass cheek. "Ready?"

Eun closed her eyes and relaxed. "Yes."

Morgan brought her hand down, cupping and lifting her flesh with a hard slap. Eun's breath hitched with the sharp sting. An equally harsh slap landed on her other cheek and a surge of wetness coated her thighs. Morgan wiped the liquid desire from her thigh with her fingertips. Eun turned her head and watched from under her lashes as Morgan brought her fingers to her mouth and licked them.

"So sweet." Morgan placed her hand on the small of Eun's back. "So wet, from just a taste of what I'm going to do to you."

Eun panted. "Do it. Now. I can't—please, don't make me wait."

Morgan pinched her ass. "So. Damn. Impatient." Morgan pinched her, punctuating her words before she drew back her hand, and then she paddled Eun's ass in earnest.

Eun clung to the table and breathed into the pain, caught up in the wild ride of surrender, giving over to the endorphins that surged through her body.

Morgan stopped and smoothed her callused palm over Eun's skin before tickling a finger over her hard clit. Eun shuddered and gasped. "More."

Morgan slapped her ass once on each cheek, forcing a cry from Eun. "More of this?" She flicked her clit and Eun whimpered. "Or more of this?" Morgan teased one finger inside and stilled her motions. "Or this?"

Eun jutted her hips back and spread her legs wider and groaned. "I don't. I don't know. All of it."

"Tell me. Ask for what you want." Morgan cracked her ass again. Eun cried out. Hot pain washed over her and morphed into a searing desire that left her gasping as tears rolled down her cheeks.

Eun groaned and rocked her hips, needing more, desperate for Morgan to possess her body and soul. "Fuck me. Please. Now. I need you inside me. Please." Tears wet the table under her face as they puddled beneath her.

Morgan lay over her, slid three fingers in, and thrust them in and out as she jacked Eun's clit in time with her strokes. Eun screamed her release as she came hard and fast. She cried out with each thrust and sank into the delicious sensation of being taken, owned, loved, even if were only for this moment.

Chapter Eighteen

Eun hugged herself as she surveyed the charred ruins of her family home. The garage was the only building standing after the fire. A sharp chemical stench wafted to her from the blackened bricks and rubble of the house. Bright-yellow caution tape blocked off the footprint of the building and an arson investigation warning sign was posted on the one wall that remained.

As the garage was situated at the back of the lot, the flames from the house had not jumped to its roof. Eun was grateful. A small bit of her childhood had survived the blaze. Unable to enter the unsafe ruins of the home, Eun had been given permission to access the garage. Morgan arrived with Rudy on his leash. A flush stole over Eun as visions of their makeup sex flooded her mind. She shifted her feet and enjoyed the pleasant well-fucked ache in her body.

"Wow." Morgan scrubbed a hand over her head. "It went up."

Eun nodded. "It was crazy. When the firefighter broke open the door, the flames shot out and then sucked back in. I've never seen anything like that." Rudy barked and looked up at them. "I know, boy." She rubbed his ears.

"I bought some boxes." Morgan inclined her head toward her truck.

Eun shrugged. "I don't think we'll need them. I can't go in to look for anything that might have survived. It's not sound." She gestured to the yellow tape surrounding the house and the arson investigation sign.

Eun led the way down the driveway to the two-story garage. Leaves and debris hung in spiderwebs, crowding the edge of the large entry door. Eun walked to the smaller side door. She dug the keys out of her pocket, sorted through them for the garage key. She reached toward the door.

"Don't." Morgan's voice was loud.

Eun paused.

Rudy barked sharply and moved in front of Morgan. His low growl was loud.

"Don't touch anything and move away from the door." Morgan tugged Rudy's leash and drew him away from the door.

Eun's pulse sped up as she backed away.

"We need to call Mel."

Eun clutched Morgan's arm. "What are you seeing I'm not?"

Morgan gestured to the ground near the door and the scratches around the doorframe. "Someone broke in here. See how the door isn't quite closed?'"

Eun bit her lip. "Is that something the chief would have done? To inspect the garage as part of the investigation?"

"Yes, but you gave her your keys, didn't you?"

Eun sucked in a breath. "Yes. She gave them back to me yesterday when we met."

They walked to the end of the driveway. Eun dialed Mel's number with shaking hands.

"Chief Michaels."

"This is Eun Park. I'm at my father's house, and it looks like someone has broken into the garage."

"Are you alone?"

"No."

"Don't touch anything. I'll be there in fifteen."

*

Mel Michaels arrived with a police officer. Eun and Morgan waited by Morgan's truck as they entered the garage. Morgan clasped her hand and squeezed gently. "Do you want to leave?"

Eun straightened her posture. "No."

The door to the garage opened, and Mel chatted with the police officer as she walked toward them.

"No one is inside, Miss Park. Things are a mess in there. Would you be able to tell if anything is missing?" The officer rested his hands on his duty belt.

Eun grimaced. "I haven't been inside since I came home."

The officer gestured to the upper story. "Most of the mess is in the attic space. There wasn't much in the garage area. Other than the car."

"My dad hated to scrape the ice off the windshield. He always kept the car in the garage." Eun shivered as a wave of grief washed over her.

Morgan stepped close and wrapped her arm around her shoulders. "Is it okay if we go in?"

The officer pursed his lips. "Not a problem with me."

Mel Michaels waved her assent. "Fine with me. I checked this out the other day."

*

Morgan led the way into the garage. The stairs leading to the upstairs loft opened to her left. She picked Rudy up and carried him up the stairs. Eun followed with her hand on Morgan's belt, desperate for her steady energy. When they entered the loft, Rudy wiggled in Morgan's arms, anxious to get free. Morgan put him down and held on to his leash.

Books and spiral notebooks were scattered and tossed everywhere. Eun's ragged breath was loud in her own ears. The love seat from Eun's childhood had been flipped over and its cushions lay about the room. Rudy sniffed and wandered around the space.

Morgan bent and picked up a few books before she stacked them on the shelves. "What do you want to do?"

Eun kneeled on the floor amid the books and torn notebooks. "Run away."

Morgan reached over and squeezed her hand. "We can. We don't have to do this right now."

Eun turned over a worn copy of *Alice in Wonderland* and closed it. She picked it up and held it to her chest. "This was my happy place as a kid. I could hide out here and read as much as I wanted in the summer. Other kids loved going to the pool. All I wanted to do was read from when I woke up until I had to go to bed."

Morgan picked up a tattered spiral notebook and passed it to Eun. "Just read?"

Eun set the book aside and took the notebook from Morgan. She flushed and looked down. "And write."

"What did you write?" Morgan stacked more books on the shelf.

"Short stories. Horribly bad poetry. The beginning of the world's worst novel."

"You still write?"

"No." Eun turned from Morgan and placed the notebooks aside. "No time. I haven't written anything not related to my job in years."

Rudy whined and scratched at the rug. His nails caught the edge of it and flipped it up.

Eun laughed. "I bet I left some snacks in there."

"What?" Morgan walked over to Rudy and slipped her fingers under his collar. "Under the floor?"

"My dad was crazy about my weight. You'd have thought I was going to be a gymnast instead of a lawyer. I used to trade doing Barb Marsh's homework for Little Debbie snack cakes. I would stash them out here and eat them when I read."

Eun crawled over to the rug and flipped it all the way back. She pushed down on the end of the flooring and a short length popped up. She slid her fingers under it and pulled it free. Morgan peered over her shoulder. A blue-and-yellow cookie tin filled the space under the wide floorboard.

Eun took the tin out and opened it. Rudy shoved his face inside the box and nosed around. He looked up, disappointment reflected in his eyes. A brown leather-covered journal was neatly centered in the box.

"Seems fancy for a kid." Morgan raised her eyebrow.

Eun took the book out and opened it. Her father's crisp Hangul covered the pages. Eun flipped to the back of the book. The last entry was two days before he had died. She closed the book and clasped it to her chest. "My dad lived alone. Why the hell did he feel like he needed to hide this out here?"

Morgan rubbed the back of her neck. "Seems weird. He must have believed it was valuable enough to hide it."

"That goes without saying, but why?" Eun chewed the end of her nail. "My dad had been taking a bunch of cash out of the business for the last few years. There's no record of where it went. He was meticulous about money."

"Did you find any cash in the house? Like maybe he was starting with dementia and hiding it? My granddad did that. We found thousands of dollars in small bills stuck in books all over his house after he passed. Maybe that's why he hid his journal."

"I didn't find any cash in the house, but I wasn't looking either. If he hid money in the house, it's gone now." She gripped the book tighter. "All of his other journals were in a plastic storage bin in a closet."

Morgan sat down and pulled Rudy into her lap and rubbed his ears. "Gone too."

"No. The bins are in the back of my car. I wanted to read them. Later."

Morgan touched her fingers to Eun's arms. "What now?"

Eun swallowed on a dry throat. "We don't tell anyone about what we've found, and I'm going to read this."

Chapter Nineteen

Morgan poured Eun another cup of coffee and one for herself. After they had arrived home with Eun's father's journal, she had read curled up on Morgan's couch, her expression alternating between confusion and outrage with occasional flashes of sadness. Sensing Eun's desire to read alone, Morgan had focused on cleaning up the second bedroom in her apartment to make room for Eun's things. She slid the single bed and a nightstand to one side of the room. Satisfied with the arrangement, she carried the rest of the bins from the living room and placed them against the wall.

A pitiful groan from the living room drew her from the bedroom. Eun was sitting with her hands over her face and rocking back and forth.

"Hey." Morgan sat next to her, looped an arm around her shoulder, and pulled her close. She stroked Eun's hair. "Maybe don't try and read all of it tonight."

Eun looked up her eyes dark. "He was fucking her."

Morgan sat up straight and stared into Eun's eyes. "What? Who her?"

"Ginny. He was having an affair with her." Eun shook off Morgan's arms and stood. She paced the room. "That fucker. So perfect. Hated me because I was a sinner. And here he was an adulterer. Fucking the damn pastor's wife!"

Eun's shout made Rudy scrunch under the coffee table. A sheepish expression crossed Eun's face. "Sorry. I hope I didn't yell loud enough for the neighbors to hear."

"You're good. The walls are thick, and Missus Johnson is visiting her sister."

Eun grabbed her hair with both hands. "I can't believe it. He puts me out of his life, and he's fucking a married woman."

Morgan stood up. "I'm sorry. And I'm sorry you found out this way. Do you think Ginny set the fire?"

"I don't know. Do you think she'd risk going to jail over being outed? And my dad's dead so who would tell? I sure as hell don't want anyone to know." Eun covered her face with her hands.

"Her husband's church is huge, and she'd lose access to all that tax-free cash." Morgan rubbed her chin. "Maybe she thought you'd tell her husband out of spite?"

Eun sat down on the couch next to Morgan. "My head hurts thinking about this. I don't want to share this with the investigator. It would make this a bigger mess."

"It would. And you don't have to decide tonight."

"Thanks for letting me crash here and giving me a place to put the boxes. Who knows what else is in his journals?" Eun winced. "I can't believe it. If I hadn't read it in his own handwriting, I wouldn't have believed it. Of all the women in the world, he picks a woman with a voice like syrup and a 1980s Laura Ashley obsession." Eun pressed the heels of her hands to her eyes. "A married woman. I mean what the fuck, Dad?"

"Explains her sobs at his funeral. I thought she was trying to outdo your aunt."

Eun sighed and leaned back on the couch. "My head hurts, and I'm hungry."

"We skipped lunch." Morgan rubbed her thumb over Eun's knee. "What do you want to eat?"

"It's Sunday, right?"

"It is." Morgan stood and stretched.

"Can we get chicken from Mai's?"

"You got it."

*

The smell of *gochujang* made Eun's mouth water. She bit into her chicken and chewed slowly. The spice of the chili exploded over her tongue. She moaned softly. "This is exactly like when I was a kid. So good." After another bite of her chicken she wiped her mouth. "I'm so glad she kept this. We had it every Saturday after my mom left. I've tried to make it myself. I can't get it to come out right. The only other place I've found it close to this good was on Oahu."

Morgan sipped her tea. "It's one of my favorites. The kimchi fried rice is amazing too. I hadn't had it until Mai added it to the menu."

Eun scooped up the fried rice and spooned it into her mouth. "I bet she makes the kimchi herself."

Morgan picked up a Hoisin-glazed short rib from her plate and waved it in Eun's direction. "I wish she'd bring back her mom's chicken long rice. That was magical."

Eun glanced around at the packed dining room and the line of patrons waiting for seats. "It's as busy as when I was growing up." She wiped her hands on her napkin. "My dad always used Mai's folks as an example of succeeding in business."

Morgan sat back in the booth. "Your dad and my dad sound the same. My dad thinks my sister and my brother are fools for not having their own businesses." Morgan rolled the edge of her napkin. "What would you have done if you could have done anything?"

Eun took another bite of chicken and chewed slowly before she answered. "I don't even know. Isn't that sad? I went along with everything my dad said I was going to do."

"What about when you were little? Like really little?"

Eun laughed. "I did want to be a dinosaur at one point, my dad used to tell me that." A wash of grief and flash of memories filled her mind. Her chest ached.

Morgan reached out and touched the back of her hand. "I didn't mean to make you sad."

Eun turned her palm up and clasped Morgan's fingers. "It's okay. It's like these grief rocks fall out of the sky randomly. I don't even know what triggers them. I'm still so mad at him, and I miss him. I've missed him for the last five years."

A shadow fell across the table. "Miss Park?" Mel stood next to their table. "I thought it was you. I wanted to see how you were doing." Her gaze settled on Eun and Morgan's clasped hands. "I see you're doing fine."

Morgan flexed her hand to release Eun's. Eun held tight to her hand and glanced up at the firefighter. "Hello, Chief Michaels."

"Hey, Morgan." Mel tilted her head and raised her eyebrow at Morgan. "How is Marilyn?"

"Wouldn't know. I haven't seen her."

Eun squeezed Morgan's hand. "Morgan's been very helpful."

"I bet."

"Michaels, order ready," Noah called from the counter.

"That's me. Enjoy your evening."

Morgan sighed. "I don't know what that was about."

Eun smirked. "She was trying to see if I was serious about you and trying to sabotage you. Scare me off. She doesn't know how stubborn I can be."

"I'm not a player. Never have been."

"I know. I knew when I met you. Unlike our friend Chief Michaels. I don't think she's used to being told no."

Morgan laughed. "She's a legend. I don't think she's ever had anyone she seriously courted say no. That uniform is a woman magnet."

"She's not you, Morgan." Eun's gaze locked on to Morgan's face. "And I don't scare easy."

*

Eun placed her purse on the kitchen table.

Morgan leashed Rudy. "I'll be a bit. Do you want to come with?"

Eun stretched. "No. I want to sit for a minute."

"Back soon."

Eun strode down the hall to the room her suitcase was in. She kneeled and unzipped the bag. Laundry. She'd have to wash her clothes soon. Not counting on seduction, or even wanting to have sex with anyone other than herself, she had not brought any sexy clothes or lingerie. She settled for a tank top and French-cut lace underwear.

After a quick shower, Eun folded down the sheets on Morgan's bed and stacked the pillows against the headboard. She leaned back against them.

The sound of Rudy's paws clicking on the linoleum of the kitchen and Morgan's low murmur to him made her heart squeeze. Morgan's footsteps in the hall drew Eun's attention, and she closed her eyes as she listened to the sounds of Morgan entering the bathroom and her footsteps on the floor when she emerged a few minutes later.

Eun opened her eyes.

Morgan was leaning against the door. "I like how you look in my bed."

Eun patted the mattress. "I'm lonely over here."

"I want a shower. I'll be quick."

Eun crossed her arms. "Hurry up, my motor's running."

Morgan snort laughed. "Give me five."

Eun folded her arms behind her head. Her body hummed with anticipation. She closed her eyes, lowered her hand, and rubbed the outside of her panties and the hardness of her clit.

"Hey, save some of that for me." Morgan launched herself from the foot of the bed and lay over Eun. She caged her in her arms. Eun drew her hands over the smooth curves of Morgan's ass and arched her hips to grind against her. Morgan nuzzled her neck. Eun lifted her chin to give Morgan access to her throat. Morgan relaxed her arms and lay over her, her weight pleasing as it pressed Eun down into the mattress.

Morgan slid her hands down her sides and edged her fingers under Eun's tank top. "You're making me feel underdressed." She shoved the tank up and lowered her mouth to Eun's breast, nibbling the undercurves before she kissed a trail up to her nipple. After sucking Eun's nipple between her lips, she circled her tongue around the tip. She worked the wet lace down her legs. Eun shifted and wiggled, lifting her hips as Morgan pulled her panties free of her body.

Eun groaned. Morgan's hands and mouth were everywhere. She wrapped her legs around Morgan's waist and locked her ankles together. She rocked against her, seeking contact to relieve the ache in her clit. Morgan growled low in her throat and ground her hips into Eun as she mouthed her breasts.

Eun clutched Morgan's shoulders, shifted her body, and rolled them over. She arched her back and pushed her breasts onto Morgan's face. "That's so good. You make me hungry." She pulled away from Morgan and captured her wrists, one in each hand. She held them close to Morgan's body as she licked and nibbled her way down her body, taking small kisses and sips of her skin. She paused to kiss the shallow turn of her hips before she nibbled the dips and curves of her body until she reached the apex of Morgan's thighs. Morgan flexed her arms, pulling against Eun's grip. "Be still. Let me." Eun inhaled the salt sweet scent of Morgan's skin, rubbing her face against the brush of soft curls over her clit. "I love the way you smell. I'm starved for you. Open your legs for me."

Morgan spread her legs and Eun nestled between them.

Eun relaxed her grip on Morgan's wrists and kissed the inside of her thighs. "Wider. Let me in."

Morgan moved her legs farther apart. Eun pressed her palms to the inside of Morgan's legs and licked a slow trail over her slick labia. A burst of sweetness spilled over her tongue. She covered her with her mouth and suckled her clit. Pursing her lips, she teased the hood back and touched her tongue to the stiff tip.

Morgan panted, her body trembling as Eun took her time and painted her clit with precise strokes of her tongue. The muscles in Morgan's body were hard under Eun's hands. Morgan arched up into her mouth and came with a long slow groan. Eun hummed her satisfaction and then licked lower, thrusting her tongue deep to taste the salt honey flowing from Morgan's body. "I love the way you taste," she murmured against her skin.

Morgan tugged at her hair. Eun wiped her face on the sheet before she slid along Morgan's body, dragging her hard nipples over her body as she did, shivering at the sensation.

Morgan cupped her face and kissed her. The taste of her orgasm flavored their kiss. Her languid kiss left Eun desperate for more. Eun rested on her forearms and lifted her head to stare into Morgan's dark eyes. Her pupils wide, a light rim of golden brown shone around the edges.

"Come over me." Morgan's husky voice sent a rill of excitement through Eun. She latched her hands on her hips and urged Eun up until she straddled Morgan's chest. The bed shifted with her movement and she grabbed the headboard to steady herself. Morgan's warm breath tickled her thighs. And she glanced down. Morgan's eyes burned with desire.

"Let me have you." Morgan raised her head and pressed her nose into the fine wet hairs over her clit before she kissed each thigh with reverence. She wrapped her arms around Eun's hips and tugged her nearer before she closed her mouth over her clit.

Morgan's arms held her locked in place as the silk heat of her tongue flicked over and around her clit. Each caress made Eun arch her back and grind against Morgan's face. Her tongue was everywhere, inside her, circling her clit and then back again, relentless as she took Eun close to the edge and held her there, holding her orgasm out of reach.

"Don't tease, give it to me. Don't stop. Take it. All of it. Me."

Eun bit her lip as the echo of her words died away in the small room. Morgan hummed as she took Eun over the edge and down into the depths of pleasure. Eun's knuckles ached where she gripped the headboard. Unable to stop, she thrashed her hips, driven by Morgan's mouth, seeking everything she wanted, everything she needed, everything she didn't dare to hope for.

*

Morgan held tight to Eun, kissing and licking her, savoring the taste of her release. Eun rose up and shifted away from her, lay on her side. Morgan scooted close and pulled her into her arms. Eun kissed her gently on the corner of her mouth and curled into her, winding her arms around Morgan's neck.

The heat between them eddied and morphed into a sweet afterglow. With one hand, Morgan reached down and pulled the covers up and over them. Morgan used her fingers under Eun's chin and lifted her face to see into her eyes. "I'm crazy about you. I don't know what you want, but I hope it's me. That you meant what you said."

Eun played with the edges of Morgan's hair at the back of her neck. "I don't say things I don't mean, Morgan. My life's a shit show right now. I don't have any idea what the hell I'm going to do, but the one thing I do know is I want to see where this goes with you."

Morgan tightened her arms around her and whispered in her ear. "We don't have to know anything more than that."

Rudy woofed softly, drawing their attention. He rose up on his back paws and placed both front paws on the bed and woofed again.

"We've talked about this, Rudy." Morgan rolled over and rubbed Rudy's head.

He whined and his deep-brown eyes fixed on Morgan's face and he woofed once more.

"All right." She patted the bed, and he jumped up. He made three circles and curled up on the blanket at the foot of the bed.

"You're so easy." Eun flattened her hand on Morgan's stomach and kissed her neck.

"I know." Morgan settled against Eun's side and ducked her head, avoiding Eun's eyes.

Eun rose up on her elbow. "Hey." She lifted Morgan's chin with her fingertips. "Look at me."

Morgan lifted her gaze.

"I'm serious, Morgan, about you, us. I'm not a user."

Morgan pressed her lips in a firm line. "I know. And it's fine whatever happens."

Eun brushed her mouth over Morgan's and spoke against her lips. "Don't write us off. Isn't that what you told me?" Her gaze burned. "I'm committed to more with you." Eun smoothed her hands over Morgan's shoulders. "We have so much to learn about each other."

Morgan twisted a lock of Eun's hair around her finger. "We do. And I should have asked if it was okay for Rudy to sleep with us."

Eun shrugged. "I've never had a dog. I don't have strong feelings about it."

Rudy's soft snores floated up from the foot of the bed.

Morgan raised her eyebrow. "You might after tonight."

"A small price to pay to sleep next to you."

"You are one smooth talker." Morgan lifted her arm and Eun cuddled closer. "I wouldn't have been able to sleep if you had stayed anywhere else after what Mel told us.”

Eun laced their fingers together. “When do you have to work tomorrow? Do we need to set an alarm?”

“No. We have a furry four-legged alarm clock.” She reached up and turned the bedside light off before she pressed a kiss to Eun’s forehead. She shifted to her side, and Morgan curled behind her, draping her arm over her waist. Eun hooked her leg over Morgan’s thigh and leaned back against her body. Her breathing evened out as she fell asleep. Morgan settled into the sensation of having Eun in her arms and in her life. She held tight, determined to keep hold of their fragile bubble of connection for as long as she could.

Chapter Twenty

Eun shoved her hair back with both hands and stared at her computer screen. Being locked out of her work email account was not unexpected, but she couldn't believe her phone calls to Heather went unreturned. Not that she wanted talk to her anyway, but what the fuck? Fifteen years with a firm, and now it's like she didn't exist?

She had dropped her security badge in the mail this morning, signed off on the final paperwork, and now, Eun was officially unemployed. A quick check of her checking account confirmed the firm had paid her out. Eun took her time and paid the few bills she had. She chewed her lip as she navigated the post office site to extend her mail hold. *When should I go back? Would she go with me? And then what? Or stay here and play house? The house is a total loss. Rebuild it? Make it mine? Start my own practice?* Eun selected a date two weeks ahead and confirmed it. The coffee pot chirped as it clicked off. After closing her laptop, Eun poured herself a cup of coffee.

She leaned back against the counter. The scuffed leather cover of her father's journal reflected the overhead kitchen light. Eun placed her coffee on the table. A bit of coffee sloshed over the side. Eun dabbed at the puddle with a napkin. She dried her hands before she touched the smooth leather of the book. After another gulp of coffee to fortify herself, she opened his journal and continued reading.

The hum of the refrigerator was loud in the small kitchen. The words ran together, and tears threatened when Eun read her father's account of their last bitter conversation. His diary ended three-quarters of the way through the journal. His final entry was filled with bland comments about the weather on a walk he had taken with Rudy. She set the book aside and topped up her coffee. Rudy padded into the kitchen and looked up at Eun. He yipped sharply.

"You need to go out?"

Rudy ran in a circle around the table, barking and yipping. He skidded on the linoleum, and his shoulder clipped the table leg. The table shifted and the journal fell to the floor facedown. Eun crossed the kitchen and picked the journal up. Writing on the last pages caught her attention. Two columns of figures marched down the page, one with dates and dollar amounts in the other. Eun blinked. Rudy's insistent bark drew her attention, and she left the book on the table.

After clipping his leash on she took him for a quick walk. Eun nibbled her lip. "Come on, Rudy. Hurry up. I'll bring you out for a long walk later." Rudy cast a baleful look at her before he followed her back inside. In the apartment Eun unclipped his leash and hung it up.

Eun flipped the journal open and ran her finger down the row of figures. The last date entered was two days before his final journal entry. She walked back to the bedroom and opened the other bins. She unpacked his other journals and stacked them next to her on the floor. She flipped through them. In each of them, on the last pages she found similar lists. Eun closed the books and replaced them into the bins. She pinched the bridge of her nose. *More mystery. And does it matter? Whoever burned the house down would think his journals had burned. But maybe that wasn't the point. Maybe someone wanted me to leave town? Like I'm going to stay. But what if I stayed? Opened a practice here and then what? Would I be happy? Bored?*

Eun flushed. The lie she had told Morgan clawed at her throat. She had tossed her dream of being a writer along with most of her old spiral-bound notebooks full of ridiculous prose when she left for college.

The bright goal of making partner had dimmed. The sharp clear path she had planned out was now a murky vision, and she had no idea how to clear the glass. Eun had time and money to do whatever she wanted to do. A heady wave of freedom washed over her, and she sat down hard on the kitchen chair.

*

Rudy brushed against her leg. She reached down and rubbed his fur. "What should we do, Rudy?" For the first time in her life she didn't have a plan, nothing to work on, nothing to do other than to wait for the insurance adjuster to call. The coffee pot shut off with a loud click. Morgan had left for work after a delicious quick fuck, and Eun's body still resonated from her touch.

She needed to talk to Ginny and had no idea how she was going to look her in the eye. She had loved Eun's dad. That was clear from her cards and letters her father had saved meticulously and added to his journals. Eun's father's journal entries were revealing. As weird as it was reading his words, Eun could not resist the lure of knowing her father in way he never would have allowed when alive.

Eun had finished the most recent journal and was now working her way back through the logs in reverse chronological order. From his words she grew to understand that his journals were his safe space, a nonjudgmental place to write down his thoughts, fears, and desires. The last few entries were the hardest to read. He had intended to reveal his affair to Eun when she visited him.

It was the nagging question of why he had decided to tell Eun about his affair that drove her crazy. Would he have apologized? Tried to make up for pretending Eun didn't exist for the last five years?

Eun shoved back from the table. Shower, and then she'd figure out her life. A niggle of worry about refusing Roz's job offer buzzed around the base of her brain. It would be the responsible thing to do. The most logical. Or would it? Eun had the luxury of money and time to figure out what she wanted to do with the rest of her life. A life with Morgan? Wasn't that the million-dollar question? Eun stretched and walked back to spare room and gathered her clothes to wash.

Rudy padded along behind her. The emptiness of her day loomed ahead of her as she loaded the washer. "We are not going sit around and mope. Come on." She picked up his leash and her jacket. "Let's go, boy."

Rudy scampered down the stairs ahead of Eun. They turned the corner and followed the sidewalk until they got to the door of Morgan's shop. Eun pushed the door open, and they entered.

"Well, hello there, Rudy," Charles called. Rudy tugged at his leash until Eun released him. He trotted over to Charles who leaned down and scratched behind his ears. Charles glanced up at Eun. "What are you two up to today?"

Eun placed both hands on the counter. "I don't know." She shrugged. "I don't have a plan."

"Morgan's going to be out all day with an install."

"She told me."

Morgan's father leaned back on his stool behind the counter. "Sometimes when you're used to doing all the time, it's super hard to sit and wait."

Eun chewed her lip. "That it is."

Charles scrubbed a hand over his bald head. "We have a great library if you like to read, and there's the dog park. Rudy likes it a lot."

"Dog park it is." She tugged on Rudy's leash. "Come on, Rudy."

Rudy sat. Eun rested her hands on her hips. "You want to stay here?" Rudy lay down with his head between his paws. Eun handed the leash over to Morgan's dad. "Seems he wants to hang out with you."

"It's fine. I like the company." Charles unclipped Rudy's leash and placed it under the counter.

"I'll come back and pick him up later."

"No need, Morgan has to come back to the shop. She can pick him up then."

"What's Morgan's favorite dinner?"

Charles cocked an eyebrow. "You a cook?"

"Not really but I don't have anything else to do today."

He rubbed his fingers over his chin. "She's not particular. Her mom's chili is her favorite."

Eun pursed her lips. "Anything easier?"

Charles laughed. "Honey, whatever you make she'll love it. The only home cooking she gets is when she comes to Sunday dinner."

"Point taken. You sure it's okay to leave him here?" She inclined her head toward Rudy.

"More than okay."

Eun waved and left the shop.

*

"Eun Park? Is that you?" Yvonne Li called from the bar of Ohana's.

"It is."

Yvonne waved Eun to her. "Thought I had missed you. I heard about your father. I'm sorry."

Mai pressed her lips. "Me too."

Yvonne tilted her head to the side. "Want to have lunch with me? Unless you're meeting someone?"

"No. I—Morgan is working."

Yvonne arched an eyebrow. "I'd heard that too."

Eun frowned. "From who?"

Yvonne laughed. "Mel Michaels was pouting when she picked up her lunch the other day, and I asked why."

Eun flushed. "Now I remember why I like living in a big city where no one knows you."

Yvonne laughed. "I hear that. I can't do anything without my sister sticking her nose in my business. Setting me up on blind dates with farmers."

"I heard that." A voice called from the kitchen. "And it was one farmer, and you weren't complaining when she dropped you off this morning."

Eun tilted head. "Is that Mai?"

Mai Li walked out of the kitchen. "It is." She rested her hands on her hips. "Good to see you, Eun." She pinched Yvonne's arm. "And you're the same way."

"Ow!" Yvonne rubbed her arm. "Are you going to make my lunch or what?"

Mai flapped her hand at the kitchen. "It's almost ready. Eun, what are you in the mood for?"

"I was told I needed to try the eggroll pizza."

"Good choice." Yvonne shifted off the counter stool and picked up her cane. "Can we sit in a booth? My ass is not built for these bar stools."

Mai snorted. "I'll bring it out when it's ready."

Yvonne placed her hand on Eun's forearm. "Come on. I want to hear everything."

*

The blare of the smoke alarm and Rudy's frantic barking startled Eun. She ran to the kitchen. Smoke seeped from the edges of the oven. No flames were visible through the oven glass. She turned the oven off and left the door closed. Eun shoved open the window over the sink. She snatched a dish towel from its hook and wafted it toward the smoke alarm, desperate for it to stop. The alarm stopped, and the smoke cleared from the kitchen. Eun wiped her forehead with the back of her wrist. After making sure there were no flames, Eun took the pan from the oven. She wrinkled her nose at the smell. Eun placed the pan with the charred remains of what would have been a roast chicken on the top of the stove and turned on the vent fan. Rudy barked and scratched at the door as a key turned in the lock.

"Easy, Rudy." Morgan stepped into the apartment kitchen and eyed the smoking pan. "Damn, what was that?"

"Dinner."

Rudy whined at their feet. Morgan kneeled next to him and hugged him close. Morgan looked up at Eun. "Um, so I'm guessing we should go out."

Eun pressed her lips together. "Sorry." The weight of failure settled over her. She couldn't even make a simple dish without a disaster.

Morgan stood up. "You okay?"

Eun opened the refrigerator and plucked out two bottles of beer. She passed one to Morgan. "Yeah. I'm not sure why I thought anything would've changed from the last time I tried cooking."

"My mom gave up trying to teach me to cook after the second time I set a pan on fire making eggs." Morgan took the offered bottle of beer and snagged the bottle opener off the refrigerator. She opened her beer and passed the opener to Eun. "Where do you want to go?"

Eun took a long sip of her beer. "I wanted to eat here, to have a nice meal ready for you when you got home."

Morgan frowned. "I don't care about stuff like that. It's cool to just come home to you."

Eun studied Morgan's face. "We can't go to Mai's. I was there for lunch."

Morgan rubbed the back of her neck. "Lots of places are closed on Monday. There's a taco truck usually set up at the brewery on Mondays."

Eun took a long drag of her beer. "Tacos it is." She inclined her head toward the burnt remains of their dinner. "Let's give this a proper burial."

"After it cools off from the cremation." Morgan grinned at Eun.

Eun grimaced. "I'm sorry. That burnt smell will stay a while."

Rudy yipped and they both looked toward him. "What's that, Rudy? You shouldn't use the smoke alarm as a timer?"

Eun rolled her eyes. "Like I haven't heard that before. Come on. Let's go get tacos." Rudy wagged his tail, his entire body wiggling with his movement.

"Let me wash up. It was dusty as hell during the install." Morgan sauntered back toward the bathroom with her beer, unbuttoning her work shirt as she did.

Eun tilted her head to study Morgan's fine ass in her work uniform and a different hunger overtook her. She finished her beer in two long pulls before she placed the bottle on the counter.

Rudy whined.

"Shh, we'll only be a minute." Eun waited until she heard the shower running and crept toward the bathroom.

The door to the bathroom was open a bit and Eun pushed it wide with two fingers.

"Eun?"

"Who else?"

"Rudy has jumped in with me once or twice."

Eun pulled back the curtain. Streams of water cascaded over Morgan's body, rivulets of soapy bubbles tracing the fine curves and angles of her body. Eun reached out and tracked her finger down Morgan's spine. Morgan shivered. Eun delighted in her reaction. She withdrew her touch. "Hurry up."

"You hungry?"

"Uh huh." Eun leaned a hip on the counter.

Morgan shut the taps off. The outline of her form was visible behind the shower curtain. The shower rings clattered along the rod in the small bathroom. She stepped out onto the bathmat. Streams of water slid down her neck and dripped off her nipples. Eun held out a towel.

Morgan took it from her hands as a cocky grin settled over her face. "Like the view?"

"Yes. Oh yes." Eun dropped to her knees and gripped the back of Morgan's thighs. She touched her tongue to her clit. She pressed her nose against her wet curls and inhaled the fresh soap scent and under it, the faint aroma of Morgan's desire. She flattened her tongue and caressed her clit with her tongue. Morgan shifted her feet, widening her stance.

Eun looked up at her. "You better hold on to something." She took her then, devoured her, sucking her clit and driving her to orgasm. Sweet salt honey burst across her tongue. Eun indulged her ravenous desire, not stopping until Morgan pushed her shoulders weakly and begged her to stop.

*

Morgan shuddered through a second orgasm, the pleasure bordering on pain. She let go of the bathroom vanity, grabbed Eun's shoulder, and pulled away from Eun's mouth. "Enough. I can't again."

Eun pouted as she nuzzled Morgan's thigh, her face shiny, a sublime expression on her face. "I've wanted to do that all day." She stood and kissed Morgan gently before she patted her cheek.

Morgan panted and struggled to catch her breath. "You can burn dinner every night if this is how it goes."

Eun swatted her ass. "Get dressed. I'm taking you for tacos."

Morgan caught her arm and spun her around. "You're not the only one who fantasized all day." She backed Eun against the bathroom door and leaned into her. With one hand she popped the button on Eun's pants and slid the zipper down. Eun scrabbled at her back. Morgan shoved past the waistband of her briefs into the silky wet heat between Eun's legs. She teased her fingertips over her thick clit before she pushed lower. Morgan groaned as she entered her searing heat. "You been like this all day?" Morgan licked and nibbled her neck and teased her finger in and out. "Thinking about me all day? How much you wanted to have me?"

Eun lifted her leg and wrapped it around Morgan's hips, pulling her close. "Shut up and fuck me."

Morgan thrust three fingers deep and ground the heel of her hand against Eun's clit as she pumped her fingers in and out. "You want this? Me to fuck you?"

Eun growled and rocked against Morgan harder. "Take it. All of it."

Morgan rocked on, slamming into Eun until she came with a shout, her nails digging into Morgan's bare skin.

Eun lowered her leg to the floor, her body pulsing around Morgan's fingers. Curling her fingers forward, Morgan stroked over Eun's sweet spot as she kissed her, swallowing Eun's soft cries as she shuddered through another orgasm.

She held tight, slowed her thrusts, cherishing her response as Eun's body throbbed around her fingers. Morgan closed her eyes and savored the sensation of Eun in her arms.

*

"Do you collect these? This is exquisite." Eun picked up a wooden puzzle box from the corner shelf. On the lid of the box, a marquetry hummingbird sipped nectar from a flower, the design created by the intricate inlays of different shades of wood.

"Some. I made that one."

"You made these. All of these?" Each one was unique in shape and design. Eun fiddled with the hummingbird box trying to figure out how to open it.

"Most of them on those three shelves."

"Why puzzle boxes?" Eun turned the box in her hand.

"Did you ever see that movie, *Hellraiser*?"

"Vaguely. Demon in a box? Or something like that?"

Morgan laughed. "That's the one. I saw it and became obsessed with puzzle boxes."

Eun tilted her head. "I take it without the demons and alternate universe?"

Morgan laughed. "Yeah. Demons not included." She held out her hand. "Let me show you."

Eun placed the box in her hands.

"It's not as hard as it looks." Morgan pressed and turned the box, sliding the sides back and pushing different areas in a sequence. After a small series of clicks it opened. She closed the box back and held it out to Eun. "You try."

Eun took the box back and turned it in her hands. "You are so very clever, and this box is gorgeous. Do you sell them?"

"No. It's a hobby."

"You should." Eun waved her hand over the shelves of polished wood boxes. "They're works of art."

"Now you sound like Dale and Eli."

"Who?" A wave of jealousy swept over Eun, and she struggled to smooth her expression.

Morgan rested her hands on her hips, the smirk on her mouth letting Eun know she had failed to keep her feelings secret.

"Dale Miller, she's a general contractor. Her dad makes guitars and mandolins. He lets me use his shop. They're always after me to sell them."

Morgan turned away and trailed her fingers over a square box. She picked it up and held it out to Eun. "This one is one of my favorites." She manipulated the box and it became a heart shape. She opened it. Inside was a small portrait of a harlequin Great Dane.

Eun glanced up at Morgan. "Who's that?"

Morgan stroked her fingers over the photo. "Beau. He was an amazing dog. Eli made this for me." Morgan manipulated the box and returned it to its square shape before she replaced it on the shelf.

Eun rested her fingertips on Morgan's arm. "Why not sell them as part of the lock shop inventory? Or sell online." She placed the box she held back on the shelf.

"I don't know. It's kind of a private thing. It would feel weird sharing them with everyone."

Eun squeezed Morgan's arm. "Thank you for showing them to me." She cupped Morgan's face and pressed a kiss to her cheek.

*

"So, you want to hear my crazy idea?" Roslyn's voice was loud in Eun's ear, and she pulled the phone away from her face.

"Hello to you too." Eun shifted on the bed and squinted at the phone's time display. Morgan had left for work before dawn, and Eun had crawled back to bed and pulled the covers up over her head with Rudy's warm comfortable weight over her feet.

"I think we should open a practice together."

Eun sat up and raked her hair back with one hand. "What?"

"Let's do it. We have the experience. We can do this. We wouldn't have to chase partner anymore. We would own the practice. We work well together. What do you think?"

Eun fell back on to her pillow and pinched the bridge of her nose. "What do I think? I think I'm too sleepy to talk about this now."

"Come on, Eun. What do you have to lose?"

"A bunch of money."

Rosslyn's snort through the phone was loud. "How can we not make money?"

Eun rubbed her eyes. "Overhead, office space, we still have to pay salaries and rent even if we're not making any money."

"Fine. But I am going out on my own, Eun. Come with me. I've missed working with you. And folks would come to us. Your clients have already been calling me to see where you are. They hate working with the new guy."

Eun chewed her lip. She was touched her clients were looking for her. Guilt at leaving them behind gnawed at her. Her clients had trusted her, counted on her. And here she was playing house and burning chickens. And having the most amazing sex and feeling cherished for the first time in her life.

"Eun? You there?"

"Yeah. Roslyn, I love you, but I can't commit to anything right now. I don't know what I'm going to do."

"What do you mean?"

"I mean I don't know. I can't get my head around anything right now."

"The sex is that good?"

Eun huffed. "It's not that. I told you. It's everything. I've never done anything for myself my whole life. I want to see where this goes. While I can. It might not go anywhere but she looks at me the way Jeff looks at you."

"You're in love with her."

Eun groaned and fell back onto the mattress. "Yes. Damn it. I don't know what to do. I'm so out of control. I can't concentrate. All I can think about is when I can have her in my arms again. I'm so fucked."

Roslyn laughed. "Aw, honey, enjoy it. And don't worry. I'm not going to do anything drastic until after the New Year. And even after, you'll always have a place with me if and when you want it."

The unspoken "when it ends" hung between them. Eun closed her eyes. "Thanks."

"Talk to you later."

Eun placed her phone back on the bedside table. She snuggled back under the covers. Rudy stalked up the bed and nosed her hand. She petted him absently. All her education had prepared her for was to work. She had no idea what to do with herself. She had been unable to come up with an answer when Morgan had asked her if she had any hobbies the night before.

Unless you counted mindlessly binge-watching shows when she couldn't sleep Eun didn't have anything she did in her spare time, because she never had any spare time. Until now. The insurance adjuster had been prompt, the claim would be paid out by the end of the month. Eun had no reason to stay in Sikesville except for Morgan and her desire to be with her.

How did one go about reinventing oneself? Eun didn't know, but she did know lying about with a dog, no matter how comforting, was not getting her any closer to figuring what to do with herself. She grimaced as she recalled her disastrous attempt at cooking. Something different today. The library. And she'd pick up a rotisserie chicken and some salad greens for dinner.

Chapter Twenty-One

"Go get it!" Morgan tossed the squeaky ball across the dog park. Rudy turned, a blur of brown-and-white as he chased the yellow toy. A puff of wind ruffled the tall weeds along the park fence. Rudy snapped the ball up and ran back to Morgan. He ran straight for her, stopped a few feet away, squeaked the ball twice, and ran away from her across the field, squeaking the ball as he ran.

Eun giggled. "He cracks me up the way he looks dead at you and then squeaks the ball, like 'I got it and you can't have it.'"

Morgan waited for Rudy to make another lap with her hands on her hips. He slowed to a walk and then placed the ball at her feet. His tongue lolled out of his mouth, and the devil was in his eyes.

"He does it to see if I'll chase him."

Eun crossed her arms. "And you don't? Because he'd outrun you?"

"No. I want him to understand I'm not going to chase him. If he wants to play, he has to come to me. I'm not going to run after him so he can make a fool of me, running away when I get close."

Eun crossed her arms. "We're not talking about the dog, are we?"

Morgan turned to Eun. "Maybe not."

"I need to go home, Morgan, if for no other reason than to figure out what my next step is. I can't think here."

Morgan picked the ball up and tossed it for Rudy again. "You taking Rudy with you?"

Rudy took off after it. And Morgan shoved her hands in her pockets to keep from balling them into fists.

"No. He loves you. And your dad. He's had enough transitions for now."

"You going to call the shelter and tell them? That you're letting him go?"

Eun pushed her hair back with both hands. "I'm not leaving you. I'm going home for a bit. I need to make a good decision. I can't stay here on a whim. I can't let everything I've ever worked for go, just because—"

Morgan spoke over her, not wanting to hear Eun call their time together a mistake, unwilling to hear their relationship described as a distraction and a diversion in Eun's life. "I get it. I wasn't trying to screw up your life, or anything." She pressed her lips together in a hard line and stalked away from Eun. Morgan swallowed the bitter taste of all the things she wanted to say to Eun. Like how much she loved her, and they could make it work, and why couldn't they be a couple? They didn't match on paper. On the surface, no one would see Morgan as a match for someone as accomplished as Eun. But Morgan had hoped Eun had seen.

*

Eun clenched her teeth as Morgan strode away from her, annoyed with her dejected attitude and pity party. "What the hell? We can't talk about this?" she shouted.

Morgan didn't answer. She bent down and rubbed Rudy's ears. He dropped the ball at her feet and barked. Morgan picked the ball up and threw it to the far end of the dog park.

What to do? Go after Morgan? Chase her? And then what? Prolong the inevitable? Morgan crossed the field toward Rudy, hands in her pockets, her shoulders hunched. A sensation of loss swept over Eun and bile burned her throat. Would Morgan still want her if she left? Or would she move on? Scooped up by someone who wouldn't appreciate her wicked humor and gentle strength. Why couldn't she understand Eun needed to be alone for a while to figure out her life?

A loud shout and vicious barking made her start. Across the park a large gray-and-white dog and Rudy were fighting. Morgan's shouts carried over the sound of barking and yelping. Eun trembled as she ran toward the dog fight. The toe of her shoe caught, and she tripped over a large stick.

She scrambled to her feet, cursing, snatched the branch up, and charged the fighting dogs. The dog had closed his jaws over Rudy's rear leg. White-hot rage filled Eun, and she brought the branch down hard across the other dog's back. He yelped and turned toward her, snarling.

Eun struck him again as she shouted a steady stream of profanity. He circled around her, and she moved with him, keeping him in front of her. He charged, and she hit him sharply on the muzzle. Morgan picked Rudy up and cradled him in her arms.

"Get away from him, I've got Rudy," Morgan shouted.

"Get him to the car. I'm okay. I'm not going to let him follow you."

Eun charged the dog, putting him on the defensive. He snapped and snarled at the air. Eun backed toward the open gate in the fence surrounding the dog park. The dog followed her, and she used the branch to fend him off.

When she reached the gate, she poked him hard in the chest, throwing her weight behind her thrust, knocking him off balance.

Eun ran through the gate and slammed the gate shut. Panting and shaking, she flipped the lock before she threw the stick at the dog and bolted for the parking lot and Morgan's truck. Her legs ached as she ran, her breath loud in her ears. Eun opened the door and swung into the seat. Bile rose in her throat and she swallowed it down as she snapped her seat belt into place. Only then did Eun risk looking back to see if the dog had followed her. Rudy whimpered from the back seat.

"Hold on." Morgan sped out of the gravel parking lot and skidded on to the blacktop.

"You okay?" Eun swept her gaze over Morgan's body. "Did he bite you?"

"No. But he really got a hold of Rudy's leg."

Eun forced herself to look in the back seat. Morgan had wrapped her flannel shirt around Rudy's leg. Blood had soaked through in spots.

Tears welled and Eun blinked them back. "How far to the vet?"

"Ten minutes. Will you call them?" Morgan passed her phone to Eun. "It's under Julie."

Eun's hand shook as she held the phone and made the call.

"Sikesville Animal Clinic, how can I help you?"

"My dog was in a fight at the dog park. He's bleeding pretty badly."

"Have we seen him before?"

Eun held the phone away from her face. "They want to know if they've seen him before."

"Put it on speaker."

Eun held the phone toward Morgan and switched it to speaker.

"Hey, it's Morgan, and it's Rudy, and we will be there in five."

"We'll be ready. Park out back and we'll take him into the trauma bay."

The call disconnected, and Eun placed the phone on the console. Eun reached back and stroked Rudy's head. "What kind of dog was that? It was so determined."

"It wasn't a dog. It was a coyote." Morgan's mouth set in a grim line. "And he must be sick, or he wouldn't have attacked Rudy. Most of the time they keep away from people. He would have killed Rudy if you hadn't hit him. He was on us before I could do anything. I need to report it."

"I'll do it after we get there. You drive." Eun twisted in her seat to watch Rudy as Morgan made the turn on to the highway and accelerated. Rudy whimpered with the motion. "Hang on, Rudy," she whispered. "Hang on."

*

Eun braced herself as Morgan made a sharp turn into the parking lot next to a low brick building. She drove around the side of the lot. A man and a woman in light-blue scrubs held open the rear door. Eun opened her door as the truck rolled to a stop.

Morgan picked Rudy up from the seat of the car and held him close. He laid his muzzle along her neck. She disappeared through the wide gray door, and the man and woman followed her.

The door shut behind them with a loud *thunk*. Eun leaned against the truck and phoned the animal control office to report the coyote. After the call, she walked around to the front of the building. The faint smell of alcohol and disinfectant greeted her as she entered.

"May I help you?" the woman behind the counter called out.

"No. I'm here with Morgan. And Rudy."

The woman's face scrunched up into a facsimile of a concerned expression. "M'okay." The click-clack of computer keys echoed in the sparely furnished waiting area. Eun sat in one of the hardwood chairs arranged around the walls of the small room. She flipped through ratty two-year-old magazines trying to distract herself. A shiver ran through her as visions of their fight with the coyote replayed in her head. Eun tossed the magazine aside, closed her eyes, and hugged herself tight and rubbed her palms over her arms.

"Eun?"

Eun opened her eyes.

Morgan exited from behind the counter and collapsed into the chair next to Eun. "They're going to sedate him to do an X-ray and a full exam to make sure he doesn't have any other bites. Did you call about the coyote?"

"I did."

Morgan slouched down in her chair and closed her eyes. "I always check to make sure the other gate to the park is closed. I didn't this time because he's so good, he'd never run off. I didn't think about a coyote coming in."

Eun took her hand and held it in both of hers. "It's not your fault."

Morgan gripped her hand hard. "I didn't know what to do. I cracked the coyote on the nose with the leash a couple of times, but it didn't even divert his attention."

Eun brushed her fingers over the dried caked mud on her jeans. "I wanted to vomit when I hit him. I've never been so angry and frightened in my life. I thought he was going to kill Rudy."

"I'm so grateful you didn't leave." Morgan lowered her chin to her chest.

"You had the keys. And it's a long walk back to your apartment. Not that I didn't consider it."

Morgan raised her head and met Eun's gaze. "I acted like an ass walking away from you like that."

Eun cupped Morgan's cheek. "I'm not leaving you. I need some time to sort myself. Trust me, please? This is not about me wanting to end whatever this is between us. If I decide to live here, I'd still need to go back to clean out my condo, find a realtor to get it on the market, and all the other annoying things you have to do when you move."

"Morgan?" A woman in dark-blue scrubs and a white jacket called from the desk. The script embroidery on her jacket read Dr. Halliday.

Eun lowered her hand, and Morgan hurried over to the desk. "How is he?"

"I want to keep him overnight to make sure his pain is controlled and to keep him quiet. The lacerations are pretty deep, and he's going to be sore from the bruising and sleepy from the sedation we gave him to clean out the wounds. We sutured the deep ones and Steri-Stripped the others. The rest will heal on its own. We gave him some antibiotics and he'll be on them for the next ten days."

Eun placed her hand in the middle of Morgan's back. "Will he be able to come home with us?"

The woman tilted her head at Eun, raised her eyebrow, and shifted her gaze back to Morgan.

"Judy Halliday, this is Eun Park." Morgan took a half step away from Eun. "She beat the coyote off of Rudy."

Judy shoved her hands in her lab coat pockets. "He should be able to go tomorrow afternoon. Call us after nine to check. If he develops a fever, he'll need to stay longer. Even though his vaccines are up to date, we gave him another rabies vaccine because that's what's recommended."

"Thank you."

"Anytime. He'll be on home quarantine for the next forty-five days." She held Morgan's gaze. "You still have my number?"

Morgan pursed her lips. "Yes."

"Use it if you have any problems with him, day or night, or if you need anything." Judy pulled Morgan to her and hugged her quickly before she turned and walked away from them.

The hair on the back of Eun's neck stood up as she studied Morgan's face as she watched Dr. Halliday walk away. She clasped Morgan's hand. "Come on. Let's go home."

Morgan let Eun lead her out of the clinic toward her truck. A breeze rustled the leaves on the far side of the parking lot.

Eun released Morgan's hand. "How long were you together?"

"Three years." Morgan met Eun's gaze. "We're still friends."

"I gathered." Eun turned and climbed into the truck and shut her door quietly. "What happened?"

Morgan grimaced. "A Vegas bachelorette party for her best friend. Turned out her best friend wanted to be more than best friends."

"I take it what happened in Vegas didn't stay in Vegas." Eun clipped her seatbelt in place.

"Nope." Morgan started the truck and backed out of the parking space.

Eun rested her hand on Morgan's thigh. "I'm sorry."

"Don't be." Morgan turned the truck toward home.

Chapter Twenty-Two

After a long quiet ride in the truck, Morgan's jaw ached. So much she wanted to say she had not. Eun was right. It was ridiculous for Morgan to want her to stay in Sikesville. Of course, she had to go home to sort her life no matter what she decided about their relationship.

On the walk up the stairs Morgan's heart ached. She missed Rudy and preemptively missed Eun. She opened the apartment door and pushed through it. After tossing her car keys on the table, she went to the refrigerator. Cold air wafted against her skin. She held the door open and stared, not seeing. She closed it without taking anything from it.

Eun's arms wrapped around her waist, and she leaned her cheek against Morgan's back. Morgan rested her hands on top of Eun's and rubbed her thumbs over her knuckles as she relaxed into the comfort of Eun's arms.

"You hungry? I could go pick something up."

"No." Morgan patted the top of Eun's hands. Eun let her go, and she moved away from her.

Eun swept her hands through her hair and lifted it off the back of her neck before she let it fall. "I'm going to shower."

She walked down the hall toward the bathroom. Morgan poured herself a glass of water and sat at the table. The ice-cold water burned her throat. Eun's father's journal sat on the table, and Morgan rubbed her fingers over the cover. The sound of the water running drew her attention, and she finished her glass of water.

The door to the bathroom was open. "Okay if I join you?"

"Of course."

Morgan stripped and stepped into the shower. The warm spray wet her body, and she took Eun in her arms and kissed her gently. Eun took the soap and washcloth. She rubbed the soap briskly over the cloth and made a rich lather. "Turn around."

Morgan turned and braced her hands on the wall. Eun washed her back, scrubbing her skin in slow circles. She groaned softly when Eun rubbed hard over the tight muscles along her spine. Morgan relaxed under her touch. Eun reached around, and she washed her breasts. Her body pressed against Morgan's back, soothing and sweet, as Eun touched her with no agenda other than caring for her.

Morgan turned in her arms and let the spray rinse the soap off her body. She took the washcloth and washed Eun, returning her tender touches. Morgan closed her eyes and leaned her forehead against Eun's brow. They held each other, the water spilling over and around them. The water cooled and Morgan closed the tap.

Eun pushed the curtain back and stepped out. She plucked a dark-blue towel from its hook and wrapped it around Morgan before she dried her body off. "You have any massage oil?"

Morgan wiped her face with the towel. "Maybe." She opened the narrow bathroom closet. "I have this." She passed a squat brown bottle over to Eun.

Eun unscrewed the cap. "Mmm, coconut vanilla." She hung her towel up and took Morgan by the hand. "Let's go." She led her to the bed. "Lie down."

Morgan stretched out on her stomach. Eun settled herself next to her on the mattress. Her oiled hands slid over the knotted muscles of her shoulders. Morgan groaned when as she kneaded the tight spot at the base of her skull. "Damn, that's sore."

"You're tighter than a bowstring. It's not your fault. You couldn't have predicted a random coyote would attack Rudy."

Morgan turned her face to the side. "I didn't see him until it was too late. And then I panicked. I was distracted."

"You were distracted by our conversation. By me. It's hard to think when we're distracted. People don't make good decisions."

Morgan huffed out a breath. "Like you trying to decide what to do?"

Eun continued stroking her hands over Morgan's back, the effect of her touch hypnotic. "All my life I've let other people direct me. My father. Girlfriends. My employer. I want to make a good decision. I want to do the right thing. For both of us. If I move here, and I'm frustrated and unhappy, it'll spill over to our relationship."

"I know." Morgan muttered into the pillow. "I don't want you to make your decision based on what you think I want you to do."

Eun moved down and rubbed Morgan's ass, her hands cupping and squeezing the large muscles there.

"If you keep rubbing my ass, I'm going to fall asleep."

Eun laughed. "I'm okay with that. This is for you." She drew her hands down the back of Morgan's thighs and massaged her calves.

Morgan lay there, her body sinking further into relaxation. Eun hummed as she worked, the sound soothing to Morgan's ears. "That's pretty. What song is that?"

"'Arirang.' My mom used to sing it to me." Eun's voice was a whisper. "When she put me to bed."

"Do you talk to her?"

"No. It's always the same. She does the best she can, but she can't fix the past. She's been sober for more than twenty years, but I've never spent much time with her."

"Do you want to?"

Eun moved to Morgan's feet, rubbing the soles and each toe.

"That feels amazing." Morgan waited for Eun's answer, sensing her apprehension.

"I don't know. I never thought about it. Turn over."

Morgan rolled to her back and tucked her hands behind her head.

"Put your hands down by your sides."

Morgan moved her hands as Eun directed.

Eun picked up her hands and massaged each finger and then her palm. Her hair fell forward and shielded her face.

Morgan lifted her hand, tucked Eun's damp hair behind her ear, and studied her expression. Worry darkened her eyes, and a muscle worked in her jaw. "You could now. You'd have time."

"Time to get to know her so she can disappoint me again?" The bitterness in Eun's voice made Morgan's heart ache.

"She came for the funeral."

Eun grimaced. "I know. And then I bolted."

"She seemed nice at the repast."

"You talked to her?"

"Yeah, well it was hella awkward with your uncle and her, so I stepped in."

Eun looked away from Morgan's face. "I should have stayed."

"No. You didn't owe those folks anything. Not after the way your uncle talked to you. It was kinda fun staying. It annoyed the fuck out of him."

Eun laughed. "Oh, I bet it did. He's not only homophobic, he's racist as hell. You should have heard the things he used to say about Yvonne's mom, even as he devoured food from their restaurant."

Morgan rested her hand on Eun's bare thigh. "I hate him for driving you from your father's funeral."

"I should have stayed."

"Nah, don't do that. You did what was required. And sat through the wackiest church sermon disguised as a funeral service I've ever attended."

Eun smoothed her hand over Morgan's stomach. "Now I know my dad was bonking Ginny, I wonder if her husband knew. If the service was directed at his wife, a passive-aggressive way to let her know he knew."

Morgan trailed her fingers over Eun's knee. "Could've been. Do you think your pop was giving her money?"

"I don't know. I went back through all of his journals. The withdrawal entries started three years ago. But from his entries, they started their thing two years before that." She huffed out a breath. "Right after he decided he didn't have a daughter anymore."

Morgan rolled to her side and clasped Eun's hand. "I'm sorry. I'm sorry you went through that. And I'm sorry you found out about your dad's affair."

"Me too." Tears streamed down Eun's face. Morgan drew her down and settled her head under her chin. She pulled the covers over them.

"It's okay whatever you decide, Eun. Take the job offer if it's what's best for you." Morgan hugged her tight. "Lots of folks have long-distance relationships."

Eun sat up and cupped Morgan's face. She kissed her gently. "Thank you. I needed to hear you say that. I've been anxious if I left town, you would start dating again."

Morgan laced their fingers together. "I want to date you, however that looks. And I want to be exclusive."

Eun levered herself over Morgan, laid her body over her, and rested her face on Morgan's chest. "I want that too."

Morgan rubbed her hands over her back and then cupped her ass. "I've got a bunch of installs tomorrow. Will you stay until Rudy is able to be alone? Until the quarantine is over? He won't be able to go to the shop until he's cleared. If it's not what you want, I can ask my family to help."

Eun kissed her cheek. "I'll stay."

*

Eun turned the coffee pot on and dropped two slices of bread in the toaster. She read through her email while she waited for the bread to toast. A flagged urgent email from the insurance adjuster detailing the amount she'd receive for the house was at the top of the queue. The house was calculated as a total loss. She sent him a return message asking for information on companies to demolish the remains of the house and clean up the lot. Her toast popped up, and she buttered the hot slices, poured herself a cup of coffee, and sat at the table.

She thumbed through the rest of her messages, deleting most of them. She paused and opened a message from Roslyn. Pictures of her daughter decked out in her recital dress and a short video of her playing the piano made Eun wistful for her former life. Work, seeing Roslyn and family every other Saturday, the safety of being so busy she didn't have to think or feel anything. In the living room, Rudy dozed on the couch. Soft snores and occasional snorts floated into the kitchen.

Her phone vibrated and she picked it up. Her uncle. Eun inhaled a big breath and blew it out before she answered it. "Yes?"

"Whatever happened to hello?"

"What do you want?"

"I want what's mine. I want the house. I'll buy it from you."

"Too late. Burned down last week." Eun moved the phone away from her ear as her uncle sputtered into the phone.

"What?"

"Yep. Total loss." Eun sipped her coffee not even trying to hide the glee in her voice.

"Everything burned? His journals?"

"What?" Eun stilled. The small hairs on the back of her neck raised and gooseflesh puckered her arms.

"You spiteful girl. Did you set it on fire just so I couldn't have anything of his?"

"I would have to die for you to get anything I didn't give you, Uncle Max."

"You act like it's impossible."

Eun sat up straighter in her chair. "Is that a threat?"

"No. A reminder. Life is unpredictable. I'm sure your father thought he had lots of time to change his will, so you got the nothing you deserved for abandoning him."

"This conversation is over." Eun thumbed the phone off and tossed it to the tabletop. She rubbed the back of her neck. The surprise and outrage in her uncle's voice over the fire sounded genuine. His mention of her father's journals niggled at her brain. Her uncle had been aware her father kept journals, had teased him more than once about his habit.

Eun sipped her coffee and studied the dust motes floating in the sunbeam, painting the kitchen table. After a minute, she shook off her melancholy, opened her father's journal, and laid it next to his bank statements. She turned to a fresh page on her legal pad, determined to find clues to where his money had gone.

Chapter Twenty-Three

Morgan opened the door to the apartment. "Hello?"

"In the living room."

Morgan placed her lunchbox on the counter and hung up her jacket before she took off her boots.

Rudy shuffled into the kitchen and snuffled at her pants leg. She kneeled and rubbed his ears. He leaned into her touch. "What did you two do all day?"

"He slept."

Morgan looked up. Eun's hair was up in a high ponytail. She wore dark-framed secretary glasses and one of Morgan's work shirts draped her frame. "Laundry day?"

A half smile tugged the corner of Eun's mouth. "You don't mind, do you?"

Morgan stood and went to the sink. She washed her hands and dried them before turning back to Eun. She held Eun's gaze as she walked across the room. "I like this look."

In two strides Morgan crossed the room. She slid her hands beneath the shirt and rested her hands on Eun's hips. Morgan rubbed her thumbs over her hip bones. Want crashed through her as she skated her hands over Eun's silky bare skin under her fingers. She brushed her lips over her mouth.

Eun took her glasses off and placed them on the counter before she looped her fingers into Morgan's belt loops and pulled her closer. She opened her mouth and teased Morgan's lips with her tongue. Morgan moved her hands down and cupped Eun's ass as she deepened the kiss. Eun pressed closer to Morgan and opened to her, their tongues teasing each other.

Morgan slid her hands up and unbuttoned the shirt before she pushed the shirt open and exposed Eun's nipples. Moving her hands up, she circled the stiff tips with the pads of her thumbs. The scent of Eun's excitement rose between them and Morgan's mouth watered. She turned them and backed Eun up against the kitchen counter.

She broke the kiss and leaned down to swipe her tongue over Eun's nipple. Eun cupped the back of her head and held Morgan's face to her breast.

Morgan trailed a finger up Eun's thigh and pushed slowly into the heat between her legs. "So wet. Have you been like this all day?"

"Only since I put your shirt on." Eun gasped when Morgan teased a finger over her swollen flesh. Morgan grasped Eun's hips and lifted her on to the counter. Eun inhaled sharply when Morgan pushed her knees apart. She leaned back on her hands and spread her legs wider.

Morgan stepped between Eun's legs and lowered her mouth. She breathed in the scent of Eun as she gripped her thighs. She licked a slow line over her and stopped to push inside and taste the sweetness hidden within.

Eun clutched at her shoulders. "Don't make me wait. Please. I need this. You."

Morgan covered her with her mouth and circled her thick clit with her tongue.

Eun arched and pushed against her. "Oh. There. Yes. Take it."

Morgan kept her rhythm as she teased two fingers inside. Eun's legs stiffened, and she dug her nails into Morgan's shirt as she came, her hips thrusting up to press against Morgan's mouth. The sweet taste of Eun washed over Morgan's tongue and wet her chin. Her sharp gasp as she came ratcheted up Morgan's want. Impatient to have more of Eun, Morgan stood and kissed her, devouring her mouth as she tugged her hips closer to the edge of the counter. Eun shifted forward and wrapped her legs around Morgan's waist and her arms around her shoulders. She kissed her neck before she teased her tongue over the shell of Morgan's ear. "Take me to bed."

Morgan held her close and strode down the hall to her bedroom. She pushed through the door and lay Eun on her bed.

Eun shrugged out of the shirt before she scooted up the bed. She spread her legs wide and feathered her fingers over her clit. "Why are you still dressed?"

Morgan yanked her shirt free from her pants and ripped it open, the metal snaps unfastening all at once.

Eun breathed out. "I love that sound."

Morgan grinned at her and unfastened her belt. The metal clinked and jingled.

Eun closed her eyes and inhaled. "You are killing me. Please hurry."

Morgan shucked her pants and launched herself toward the bed. She settled over Eun and pressed their flesh together. Hard nipples pressing, the slick slide of her clit over Eun's wide thigh made her groan.

Eun pressed Morgan's head against her neck and reached between them. Her fingers brushed over Morgan's stiff clit. "You need something?"

"Everything." Morgan closed her eyes against the sweet pleasure of Eun touching her as she moved her hand lower and fingered her. "Fuck me. I want you inside me."

Eun thrust sharply and curled her fingers, her palm pressed against Morgan's clit as she stroked her fingers in and out. Morgan shifted her legs, opening herself as Eun rolled them so she was over Morgan.

Morgan clasped her ponytail and tugged. Eun lifted her chin and exposed her throat. Morgan kissed the smooth column. Eun groaned and thrust deeper. Morgan gasped and lost her focus as Eun took her up and over. Her body clenched around Eun's thrusting fingers and pleasure spun out from her center. Morgan shouted Eun's name as she came hard, her shoulders lifting from the bed.

Eun slowed her strokes and kissed Morgan, swallowing her cries. Morgan broke their kiss and stared into Eun's dark eyes. Eun pressed deeper and added a finger. The sting and burn gave way to pleasure and Morgan arched her hips to meet Eun's deep slow strokes. A fire built in her belly and her vision narrowed. Nothing existed except the intense pleasure between her legs and the breathtaking intensity of Eun's focus.

Eun pressed her wet flesh to Morgan's thigh. "Can you come with me?" She rode Morgan's thigh.

Morgan flexed her leg and rocked into Eun. "I don't know." She panted.

"How about now?" Eun swept her thumb over Morgan's clit.

"Yes. Oh, damn."

"Eyes open. See me. Let me see you."

Eun sped up her thrusts. "Now, Morgan, now. Give it to me. Give me everything." Eun's eyes widened as she cried out. Morgan's orgasm exploded, detonating from deep in her belly, her body and mind surrendering to Eun. And she saw. All of it. All the unsaid things between them. Nothing existed except for Eun's dark-brown eyes and the love Morgan saw reflected in their inky depths.

*

Eun smoothed her palm over Morgan's bicep and curled into Morgan's body, pressing against her back. "Do you think Rudy will be cleared to go to the shop in two weeks?"

Morgan reached up and clasped Eun's hand, pulling it to her chest. "He should be." She rolled to her back and peered into Eun's face. "When do you want to go back? I could ask my mom to come stay with him if you need to go sooner."

Eun rested her head on her palm. "I don't have a schedule, Morgan. My time is my own now."

She flattened her palm over Morgan's chest. "You said before you wouldn't mind if I stayed with you for a bit. Until I have a place of my own. Is that offer still on the table?"

"Why wouldn't it be?" Morgan's mouth drew down.

"I don't know. I didn't want to assume. And I can afford an apartment of my own."

"I know you can. But I like having you here. Rudy likes having you here." Morgan cupped the back of Eun's head and kissed her gently. "It would give you time to find a place you love instead of taking the first available apartment." She kissed Eun again, gently, before she met her eyes. "And if you decided to move back to Chicago"—

Morgan lowered her gaze—"you wouldn't be bound to a lease or anything."

Eun lifted Morgan's chin and rubbed her thumb over her lower lip. "It's a generous offer." She held Morgan's gaze. "I don't know what the future will bring, but for now I want to be here with you."

A smile tugged the corner of Morgan's mouth. "You want me to go back with you? Between my truck and your car, it'd save you renting a U-Haul."

Eun groaned. "So cliché, and you would do that? You could take time off?"

"Sure, I can. And it's only until you find a place." She rolled over until she was above Eun, her expression serious. "I mean it, Eun. I want what's best for you. If you're with me five months or fifty years, I want you to make decisions based on what you want, not because you think it's the right thing or you owe someone."

Eun hugged Morgan close and leaned her forehead against her brow. "Thank you." She swallowed around the dry ache in her throat. "I love you, Morgan."

Morgan relaxed against her and snuggled close. "I'm glad you said it first. I've been trying to figure out how to tell you I love you since you saved Rudy and me at the dog park." She kissed the side of Eun's neck.

Eun squeezed Morgan tighter. "This is a new thing for me, Morgan. I've not had a relationship in a long time. I might screw up. A lot."

Morgan kissed her neck again. "You might. But you're good at communicating. We're adults. And we both might screw up a lot, but as long as we keep talking, we can work it out."

Eun rubbed the back of Morgan's neck. "Can you see the clock?"

"Why? Do you have an appointment?"

"Very funny. I wanted to see if we still had time to order from Mai's."

Morgan rose up and kissed Eun, her tongue skating over her lower lip before she took the kiss deeper. Eun groaned and shifted her hands to Morgan's ass. She broke the kiss, panting. "Never mind. What I want is not on the menu at Mai's." She rolled her over, slid down her body, and gorged herself on the sweet feast between Morgan's legs.

*

"What'd you get?" Morgan placed her stack of books on the library table.

Eun handed a thick book to Morgan. "Celeste Quon's *Stone Gate*. Have you read it?"

"No, but Neil has been after me to read it for years."

"Did you see the movie? I was afraid to watch it, worried they'd ruined it. But it was good." Eun drew her fingertips over the edge of the binding. "I read my first copy so many times it fell apart."

Morgan pulled her library card from her wallet and checked their books out. "Want to pick up tacos on the way home?"

Eun lifted the stack of books from the counter. "You read my mind."

*

Rudy yipped sharply when they opened the door to the apartment.

"I'm sorry, bud, we weren't gone that long." Morgan held up the bag of tacos. "And we brought treats." Rudy huffed and sat down with his back to them.

Eun covered her mouth to hide her smile. "He's dissing you."

Morgan placed the bag of food on the table. "Come on, Rudy."

Rudy snuffed loudly and walked into the living room. "He's totally dissing me."

Eun opened the refrigerator. "What do you want to drink?"

"Some sparkling water would be great."

Lured by the smell of tacos, Rudy returned. Morgan tore a tortilla into pieces and placed it in his bowl.

After dinner they settled on the couch. Eun rested her head against Morgan's thigh and propped her book on her chest. Morgan carded her fingers through Eun's hair as she read, pausing only to turn the page of her book. Eun closed the book and rested it on her chest. "I don't think I've ever had a reading date with anyone."

Morgan peered down at her. "Why not?"

Eun flushed. "I've mostly read for work the last fifteen years. I used to read for pleasure all the time." She snorted. "The women I've been with weren't interested in reading. So, thank you."

"For what?"

"Encouraging me to be myself."

Morgan shrugged. "I want you to enjoy yourself and be happy. To do the things you want to do."

Eun reached up and pulled Morgan into a soft kiss. "Want me to read the sexy bits to you?"

"There's sexy bits?"

"Over the top sexy bits."

Morgan placed a bookmark in her book and set it aside. "Read on."

*

Morgan pulled her truck into the parking lot behind her apartment. She gathered her lunch box and jacket before she climbed down from the truck. A bit of glass crunched under her boot. She glanced at Eun's car. The driver side window was shattered. She peered into the car. The glove box hung open and its contents were scattered over the seats. Morgan pulled her phone from her jacket and called Eun. She laid her lunchbox and jacket on the hood of the truck. By the fifth ring her palm was sweating. She scrubbed her hand against her pants to dry it.

A panting Eun answered the phone. "Sorry, I was in the shower."

"Have you been home all afternoon?"

"What kind of question is that? And yes, other than when I took Rudy out."

"It looks like someone beat your car with a bat."

"The fuck?"

"I'll call the police."

"I'll be right down."

Morgan walked around the car taking photos with her phone. The trunk was closed but not latched. She kneeled down and looked under the car. Nothing seemed out of place. A bit of paper fluttered out of the car window. Morgan snagged it out of the air. The gravel crunched behind her and she turned in the direction of the sound. Eun rounded the corner of the car.

"Is it a receipt?" Eun gestured to the scrap of paper.

Morgan stood and smoothed it out. "A dry-cleaning ticket."

Eun frowned. "Where's it from?"

Morgan gestured at the car. "I'm guessing it fell out of the pocket of whoever busted your car up." She squinted at the numbered receipt. "This is from Sam's."

Eun raised an eyebrow. "You can tell from the number?"

Morgan shrugged. "We only have one dry cleaner in town."

"It's a generic receipt. It could've come from anywhere."

Morgan nodded. "Yeah, but Sam's done our uniform shirts forever. I would recognize his handwriting anywhere."

A police car arrived. "Hey, Morgan. What you got?"

"Hey, Martin. This is Eun Park. And that's her car." Morgan tucked the dry-cleaning receipt into her pocket.

"Ma'am." He pulled a notebook from his pocket and pointed his pen at the car. "Is the vehicle registered to you?"

"Yes."

"Have you assessed the damage?"

"We left it as it was."

After inspecting the car with them, Martin took their statements and gave Eun the information she would need for her insurance claim.

After Martin left, Eun kicked her toe against the tire of her car. "Do you think this was to intimidate me or to punish me?"

Morgan frowned. "Who would want to intimidate you?"

"Good point. I'm not working any cases where folks might want to scare me off. So, who wants to punish me?"

"I don't think they were trying to punish you. They didn't do any damage other than breaking the window, and I think they only broke it to get into your car. They tossed the car and the trunk like they were looking for something. If they wanted to punish you, they would have fucked with the engine." She pulled the dry-cleaning receipt from her pocket. "I think we need to go see Sam."

Eun raised her eyebrow. "You're a detective now? Shouldn't we call your sister?"

Morgan huffed a breath. "The police won't follow up on this. It's not a priority. Nothing was stolen. They'll treat it as a simple case of vandalism."

Eun wrapped her arms around herself. "I need a jacket."

Morgan opened her truck and pulled an empty canvas grocery bag from the back. "I'll get everything out of the car." She glanced at the sky. "I don't think it's supposed to rain. Grab a couple of trash bags from under the sink." Morgan held up a roll of duct tape. "We can use them to tarp the window."

Eun nodded, her brows furrowed. "I'll be down in a few."

Chapter Twenty-Four

The bells over the dry cleaner's door jangled when they pushed through the doors.

A short woman with a pinched face and iron-gray hair swept up in a bun stood behind the desk. She peered over her glasses. "You're early, Morgan. Your shirts won't be ready until after two tomorrow."

"I know, Alice." Morgan walked to the counter and held out the ticket to the woman. "I'm doing a favor for a friend." She held out the receipt.

"Since when are you friends with Adam Burns?" Alice shifted her gaze from Morgan and squinted at Eun.

"I'm Eunice Park. Ginny worked for my father." Eun held Alice's gaze and used her most persuasive tone. "They've both done so much for me since my father passed. I had some errands to run and offered to pick up their dry cleaning."

Alice shrugged and turned away, taking the ticket with her. The motorized rack spun and clicked to a stop. She plucked two suit coats and three shirts covered in plastic and hung them next to the register. "We couldn't get the wax stains out his pants. Tell him we tried."

"I'll tell him."

Eun paid the bill with cash. Morgan lifted the plastic-draped clothes from the rack by the cash register and hung them over her shoulder.

"See you tomorrow, Alice," Morgan called over her shoulder as they left. Outside the shop, a quiet rage settled over Eun as she stalked toward Morgan's truck.

Morgan opened the truck. "What now?"

"We deliver the dry-cleaning. And ask Adam Burns what the hell he's looking for."

"You sure that's what you want? We could call Miesha."

Eun rubbed the back of her neck. "I'm so sick of this mystery. So much drama." She turned to face Morgan. "I saw Adam the day of the fire. He was sketchy as hell."

"What? Did you tell Mel?"

"No. I didn't think of it until now."

"Did he say why he was there?"

"Some crap answer about picking up Ginny's Bible." Eun pressed her lips in a thin line. "He would have had keys. And Ginny burned one of those fat smelly jar candles on her desk all the time."

Morgan drummed her thumbs on top of the steering wheel. "It could just be a bunch of coincidences."

Eun pinched her nose. "You're right. It doesn't mean anything. He's a pastor. He probably has wax stains on his suits all the time."

"Where to now, Sherlock?"

Eun tilted her head to the side and rested her cheek on the seat. "I'm hungry. Let's grab a bite and plan. And hope Adam Burns has enough suits he doesn't go to pick up his dry cleaning in the meantime."

Chapter Twenty-Five

Mai's restaurant was packed with the evening dinner crowd and they had to wait for a table. Eun paced the small waiting area. Morgan tapped her on the shoulder. She tilted her head toward the dining area and leaned close to whisper. "Isn't that your uncle?"

Eun turned and scanned the dining area. "Oh hell. And Adam Burns." Her stomach clenched.

"Adam doesn't look happy."

Eun grimaced. "My uncle has that effect."

She squared her shoulders. "Well. At least we can confront them at the same time." Eun pushed past the diners ahead of them in line, excusing herself she went. The two men were seated at a back table. Their heads were so close they almost touched over the tabletop. Adam's hands were knotted together in his lap.

Morgan caught up to Eun and grabbed her arm to stop her progress. "Wait up. Do you know what you are going to say?"

A server brushed past Eun's shoulder. "You need to wait to be seated." She inclined her head to the front of the restaurant.

"We're looking for someone." Eun smiled at the server before she pulled free from Morgan's grasp and pressed her lips in a thin line. "No, I don't."

They arrived at the table. The two men looked up. Adam's eyes widened, and a wave of fear washed over his face before it dissolved into fury.

Eun's uncle gave her an oily smile. "Eun. How fortuitous. I was going to call you."

"Shut up." Adam's lips pulled back in a snarl. "Shut your filthy mouth."

Eun tilted her head. "Why?"

Eun's uncle opened his mouth to speak. Adam lunged across the table and wrapped his hands around his throat. Glasses and silverware clattered to the floor as the table tilted. They crashed into Eun and knocked her to the floor as they wrestled. She kicked wildly to get free from them. Morgan grabbed her arm and helped her to her feet. She pushed Eun away from the brawl.

Adam straddled Max. "Shut up. Shut up. Shut up," Adam chanted, his knuckles white as he squeezed her uncle's throat. Max's face turned red and then faded into a dusky shade of blue.

"No. Stop!" Eun screamed.

Morgan grabbed the back of Adam's jacket and tugged. Adam growled and flailed with one arm at Morgan. His wild swing clipped her jaw. Morgan let go and backed away.

The harsh sounds of Eun's uncle's struggle to breath under the assault of Adam's hands filled the restaurant. Max grabbed Adam's hand and yanked his finger back.

Adam bellowed with pain. Max scrabbled a fork from the floor and plunged it into Adam's throat. Blood spurted from his neck. He slapped the fork from his neck and grabbed Max by the collar and banged his head on the floor. A cacophony of screams and shouts from other patrons swirled around them. Chairs scraped across the floor as the other patrons scattered.

Ginny ran past Eun and barreled into both men, knocking Adam off Eun's uncle. "Stop, Adam. Stop." She clutched his face between her hands. "Stop. Please stop."

Tears ran down Adam's face. "Ginny. No. He's going to tell everyone."

She peered into his face and slid her hand down to cover the wound in his throat with her hand. Blood seeped between her fingers. "I'm sorry. So sorry. So very sorry."

Eun's uncle crawled away from Ginny and Adam. He wiped his bloodied hand on his suit coat. Eun knelt beside her uncle. A crowd of police officers filled the space.

Max pushed himself to sitting and propped himself against a booth, his face ashen. "He tried to kill me!" he rasped.

"Because you were trying to shake him down, uncle." Eun rose to her feet and gestured to the two men. She pointed at Adam. "He assaulted Mister Park because Mister Park was trying to extort money from him."

"He's an arsonist. He burned my brother's house," Eun's uncle cried out.

"He's a blackmailer. He's blackmailed his brother and my wife for years."

"She's a filthy whore who seduced my brother." Max opened the collar of his shirt exposing the livid marks of Adam's fingers. "He tried to strangle me."

Adam struggled against Ginny's hold. "Let me go."

Miesha stepped forward and blocked Adam's progress. "Simmer down, Mister Burns. The paramedics are on their way."

The paramedics arrived. Eun turned away from the scene. Morgan's arm around her shoulders grounded her as she led Eun to the back of the restaurant.

Mai passed them and nodded toward the kitchen. "Take her to the pass-through. I'll go sort this."

"Have some tea. You look like you could use it." Yvonne passed a cup of tea to Eun.

Eun took the cup with both hands. "I'm sorry about your restaurant."

Yvonne shrugged. "It's better than when the Central Catholic wrestling team started a fight with our team when we were kids. We had to replace both front windows."

"I'd forgotten about that." Eun sipped her tea.

Yvonne rested her hand on Eun's arm. "I know now is crazy, but when you have time, I want to talk with you. Before you go back to Chicago."

"Sure. I'd like that." Eun chewed her lip as her uncle was led out in handcuffs. "I didn't imagine any of this would happen."

The paramedics wheeled Adam out with Ginny following close behind. Morgan looped an arm around her waist. "No one could have predicted it."

Miesha followed behind the paramedics and stopped at the counter. "I'll need your statement, Miss Park."

Eun placed the cup on the counter. "I'm ready."

Chapter Twenty-Six

"You're happy here?" Eun leaned back in the booth.

"I am." Yvonne rested her palms flat on the tabletop. "I'm surprised after the crazy hustle of LA, but I like it here. I swore I'd never move back, or date a farmer, but here I am. So never say never." She rolled her cup between her palms. "I will confess to being bored occasionally. I don't have much to do with running the restaurant."

Eun nodded her understanding. "I'm already antsy. I miss working."

"What about Reverend Burns and your uncle? How's that going? Did you have to hand over your father's journals?"

"No. Adam refused to press any charges against Uncle Max." Eun pushed her hair back with both hands. "In the assault case, Max claimed self-defense. And because Adam had his hands around his throat when he stabbed him—" Eun chewed her lip as the images of the fight surfaced in her mind. "—Max didn't even spend one night in jail. Adam's trial isn't slated to begin until the fall. I hate thinking about having to testify."

"You get why he did it. And that makes it hard."

Eun knotted her hands together. "Yes. He loves Ginny. Even after he found out about the affair, he wanted to protect her, keep her reputation intact. I hate that the last memory of my dad for this town will be so sordid."

Yvonne patted the back of her hand. "I'm sorry. That's awful."

Eun drew back and placed her hands in her lap. "I'm working on not thinking about it."

Yvonne took a sip of her tea and peered at Eun over the edge of her cup. "So, are you planning on staying here until the trial is over or are you moving back to Chicago?" Yvonne cocked an eyebrow.

"I'm going to stay." Eun flushed. "I haven't told Morgan yet."

Yvonne leaned forward in the booth. "You looking to join a practice here?"

Eun pursed her lips. "No. If I do anything, it will be on my own. I'm through making money for someone else."

"Would you consider joining me? As part-time partner?" Yvonne inclined her head toward her cane. "I have good days and bad days. And I don't want to work full time. I hate litigating. I need a partner who would go to court if need be, so I don't have to."

Eun knotted her hands together. "I don't even know if I want to practice anymore."

"So, keep it low key. Only work as much as you want and only on the cases you want." Yvonne sipped from her water.

"I don't know anything about starting and running a practice. I've been pretty narrow in my practice focus."

"I know how to run a practice. And we can make it what we want. This town is so small a general law practice is more viable than a specialty. You can learn what you need to learn. I can help. We can make it what we want, Eun. On our terms. Your former employers were assholes to let you go. I don't want to set the world on fire, but I like to work when I can."

Eun tilted her head to the side. "You're making it hard to say no."

"So, say yes." Yvonne reached across the table and rested her hand on top of Eun's and patted it. "Come on. I want to show you something."

Eun frowned. "What?"

"Your new office." Yvonne grinned at Eun as she waved the server over to their table.

*

Morgan filled Eun's glass with sparkling water before she sat across from her. "I'm going to get spoiled as hell with you having dinner ready when I get home."

"Don't get too excited. I met Yvonne for lunch and ordered extra for dinner."

Morgan laughed before she took a bite of the sauce-covered pasta on her plate. "Where'd you eat?"

"The new place on Thirty. Angel's."

Morgan wiped her mouth. "It's good."

Eun pushed her food around with her fork. "Yvonne asked if I'd join her practice as a partner."

Morgan leaned back in her chair and her brows drew down. "What'd you tell her?"

Eun scooted her chair closer to Morgan's. "Yes."

"So, you're staying?" Morgan placed her fork next to her plate, scooted back her chair, and faced Eun. She leaned in and kissed the corner of Eun's mouth. "For real?"

Eun swayed closer to Morgan. "Yes."

"When were you going to tell me?"

"Now." Eun climbed onto Morgan's lap, caught her shirt in both hands, and drew her into a quick kiss. "You okay with that?" She searched her eyes seeking her answer, fearful of what she might see there.

Morgan traced her finger over Eun's cheek and then cupped her chin with her hand. She held Eun's gaze. "More than okay."

Morgan rested her hands on Eun's waist and leaned her brow against Eun's chest, her shoulders tense under Eun's hands. She stroked her fingers over the back of Morgan's neck. "Hey, look at me."

Morgan raised her head and peered into Eun's eyes.

"I love you, Morgan. I'm willing to try this with you. But you have to promise me one thing."

"What's that?" Morgan frowned.

"If you ever are over this, over me, you tell me straight up. No lying. No cheating. If we have a problem with each other, we talk about it."

Morgan held her gaze. "Deal. You have to promise me something too."

"Yes."

"Whatever happens, don't assume I'm going to give up on us or you." She lifted Eun's hand and brought it to her mouth and kissed her palm. "You have to promise to keep talking to me, no matter what."

"Always." Eun locked her arms around Morgan and held tight to their future.

*

Morgan polished her fingerprints off the lock. "There. You are officially secure."

Eun placed a stack of folders she was sorting on her desk. "It's beautiful."

Morgan laughed.

"Come over here." Eun crooked her finger.

Morgan stuffed the cloth into her pocket and walked to where Eun stood. Eun reached out and wrapped her arms around Morgan's neck. "Let me thank you properly." She kissed Morgan, lingering on her lower lip. Morgan groaned as Eun deepened the kiss. Gasping, she broke away. "No fair. I have another install to do. I'm going to be distracted the rest of the day."

Eun pressed against her and nibbled her earlobe. "Guess you'll have to wait until you get home."

Morgan grabbed Eun's hips and lifted her on to the desk. "Will I?" She ground against Eun and nuzzled her neck. Eun wrapped her legs around Morgan's hips. "Maybe not. Why don't you see if that lock works?"

Morgan lifted clear of Eun and crossed to the door in two steps. She turned the knob and seated the deadbolt. Eun pressed her against the door and captured her wrists in one hand. "Perfect."

Morgan relaxed into her grasp. Eun slid her hand down and plucked the snaps on Morgan's shirt open. She palmed her breast over her sports bra before she scratched her short nails over Morgan's stomach.

Morgan panted. Eun kissed the corner of her mouth as she opened her belt and slid her hand down to sweep her fingers over Morgan's clit. Morgan hollowed her stomach, giving Eun more access. Eun groaned softly. "I love how wet you get." She stroked on, relentless, and Morgan shattered under her touch. "Mm. I love how you come for me. Will that hold you until this evening?" Eun released Morgan's wrists and leaned against her.

Morgan kissed Eun and slid her hands down her tight skirt. "Maybe." She dropped to her knees and pressed her cheek against the front of Eun's skirt.

Eun used the flat of her hands and raised her skirt. Morgan nuzzled the silk of her panties, inhaling deeply before using her fingers to pull the fabric to the side. She circled her clit with her tongue before licking between her swollen folds. Eun latched onto her shoulders with both hands. Morgan pulsed her tongue in rhythm and then slid two fingers into her slick heat.

She cupped the back of Morgan's head and held her in place as she licked and sucked until Eun came undone.

*

The sun broke through the clouds and lit up the deep-green grass of the dog park. Rudy limped next to them. Eun scanned the park. The gates were secured. She worried her lip with her teeth.

Morgan touched her arm. "We're safe. I walked the entire park."

Eun unfastened Rudy's leash.

Morgan pulled a yellow tennis ball from her pocket. Rudy fixed his gaze on the ball and woofed softly. Morgan tossed the ball across the field. Rudy took two steps and sat down. He looked over his shoulder at Morgan and Eun.

"Maybe it's too soon?" Eun rubbed Morgan's arm.

Morgan patted her hand where it curled around her bicep. "Maybe."

They walked toward the ball with Rudy following them. Morgan stuffed the ball into her jacket pocket. Rudy snuffled the grass. "Maybe if we walk around, he'll see it's safe."

She took a step forward and patted her leg. "Come on, boy."

Rudy rose stiffly and walked to Morgan's side. They walked around the fenced yard, stopping whenever Rudy wanted to sniff or investigate. The squeak of gate hinges drew Morgan's attention.

"Hey Morgan, Eun."

Judy Halliday unleashed the yellow lab at her side. Rudy barked. The lab bounded across the field. Rudy barked once more and ran to meet the other dog, his entire body wiggling in greeting. Morgan and Eun to walked to meet Judy.

"I see he's feeling better." Judy tucked the leash into her pocket.

"Maisie is magic. He didn't want to play at all until he saw her." Morgan shielded her eyes with her hand, her gaze fixed on the dogs.

"Some dogs need another dog to help them remember how to play."

Eun linked her arm through Morgan's. "Not just dogs." She fished the ball from Morgan's pocket and tossed it toward the pair. Rudy caught the ball and ran in a tight circle around them before leading Maisie on a chase around the field.

Morgan ran after the dogs, a wide grin on her face as she called for Rudy to surrender the ball. Eun tucked her hands into her pockets and turned in a small circle to watch the three of them play. Rudy's sharp barks mixed with Maisie's baying and Morgan's laughter rolled over the grass toward Eun and she lifted her face to the sun.

"Morgan says you've moved here." Judy stepped up next to Eun.

"I have." Eun shifted and faced Judy.

"Will you open a practice?" Judy tilted her head to the side.

"I joined Yvonne Li. Are you looking for an attorney?"

Judy crossed her arms over her chest. "Morgan is amazing. Wonderful really." Her gaze tracked Morgan and the dogs.

Eun stifled the raw edge of jealousy that flared in her throat. She raised her eyebrow and studied Judy's expression. "I agree. She's wonderful and amazing. And your point?"

A blush spread over Judy's face and she turned to Eun. "I mean she's special. We didn't work out but—she deserves someone who knows how special she is."

Eun rested her hands on her hips and returned Judy's sharp gaze. "I'm not going to break her heart if that's what you're worried about. Or are you sounding me out to see if you've got a chance to get back together with her?"

"No. That's not going..." Judy blushed and faded out.

Morgan trotted up to them, out of breath. "That was fun. He's back to himself."

Judy stepped back and whistled. Maisie trotted over to her. She clipped the leash on her. "I've got to get going. I have a full afternoon clinic." She turned sharply and walked away from them.

Morgan turned back to Eun. "That was sudden."

"She wanted to make sure my intentions were honorable."

"What?" Morgan frowned.

Eun stepped close to Morgan. "She wanted to make sure I knew how special you are."

"Oh, for fuck's sake." Morgan snorted and quirked her mouth. "After she cheated on me?"

Eun pressed closer. "You are special, Morgan. And I'm not going anywhere."

Morgan leaned down and kissed her. A weight settled against her leg. Eun broke the kiss and looked down. Rudy sat on her foot and looked up at her. She reached down and ruffled his fur. "Let's go home."

Morgan clipped the leash to Rudy's collar and handed it to Eun. "Lead on."

Acknowledgements

I would be remiss if I didn't give credit to Crystal Hunt and Eileen Cook and their wonderful workshops/classes and advice over cocktails at Surrey International Writer's Conference. Thank you for your wisdom, humor, guidance, and encouragement.

About the Author

Brenda Murphy writes short fiction and novels. Her novel Double Six won the 2020 GCLS Goldie for Erotica. She loves tattoos and sideshows and yes, those are her monkeys. When she is not loitering on her front porch and writing, she wrangles two kids, one dog, and an unrepentant parrot. She blogs about life as a writer with ADHD and publishes photographs on her blog Writing While Distracted. Sign Up for her email list and receive free short stories at www.brendalmurphy.com

Blog: www.blog.writingwhiledistracted.com

Website: www.brendalmurphy.com

Facebook: www.facebook.com/Writing-While-Distracted

Twitter: @bmurphysideshow

Other NineStar books by this author

Dominique and Other Stories
One

The Rowan House series
Sum of the Whole
Both Ends of the Whip

Also Available from NineStar Press

Connect with NineStar Press

www.ninestarpress.com

www.facebook.com/ninestarpress

www.facebook.com/groups/NineStarNiche

www.twitter.com/ninestarpress

9 781648 901201